HIS BANANA

PENELOPE BLOOM

1

NATASHA

I made an art of being late. Unfortunate acts of clumsiness were my paintbrush, and New York City was my canvas. There was the time I didn't show up to work because I thought I had won the lottery. As it turned out, I was reading last week's numbers. I had texted my boss on the way to pick up my winnings. I told him I'd never need to attend another *should have been an email* meeting on my mega yacht, where beautiful, tanned men would be hand-feeding me grapes. Unfortunately, my boss had actually printed out the text and framed it for the office, and the only thing being hand-fed to me that night was stale popcorn... by myself.

Then there was the time I watched *Marley and Me* the night before work and couldn't stop crying long enough to make myself presentable. I'd gotten on the wrong trains, spent thirty minutes looking for keys to the car I didn't own, and once even missed dinner with my best friend because my dog was having a mental breakdown.

Yeah. I wasn't proud of it, but I was kind of a walking disaster. Okay. More than kind of. I was a chaos magnet. If there was a button you absolutely should not under any circumstances push, a priceless vase, a heart-attack-prone old man, or just about anything that can be messed up, I was probably the last person you wanted around. But hey. I was a damn good journalist. The fact that I still had a job was a testament to that. Of course, the bottom-of-the-barrel assignments I always seemed to land were also a reminder that I was permanently and irrevocably on the shit list. It was hard to get ahead when you had a tendency to accidentally shoot yourself in the foot, no matter how good your stories were.

"Wake up," I said, kicking my brother in the ribs. Braeden groaned and rolled over. He was turning thirty in a week, and he still lived with my parents. Their one requirement was that he help with chores around the house. Of course, he never did, which meant they would occasionally make the empty threat to kick him out. He'd crash on the floor of my closet of an apartment for a day or two until things blew over with them, and then he'd be out of my hair again.

If I was a functional mess, Braeden was my dysfunctional counterpart. He had all the same self-sabotaging genetics without the perseverance to fix his mistakes. The result was a twenty-nine-year-old whose primary hobby was playing Pokemon Go on his phone, who sometimes moonlighted as a "sanitation officer," which was basically a minimum-wage gig picking up trash for the city.

"The sun isn't even up yet," he groaned.

"Yeah, well, your two-day grace period is up, B. I need you to go patch things up with mom and dad so I can have my shoebox to myself again."

"We'll see. I've got a pokemon I wanted to catch while I'm downtown. Maybe after that."

I threw on my coat, settled for two different shoes—one dark brown and one navy blue, because I was out of time to keep searching—and crept through the hallway of my apart-ment. I lived across the hall from the landlord, and she never missed an opportunity to remind me how much money I owed her.

Yes, I paid my rent. Eventually. My shit list assignments weren't exactly the top paying jobs at the magazine, so sometimes I had to pay other bills. Like electricity. If I was feeling really adventurous, I even bought food. My parents weren't loaded, but they were both teachers, and they made enough money to lend me some if I was ever in desperate need. I wasn't exactly too proud to ask, but I didn't want them to worry about me, so I swore Braeden to secrecy on the bare contents of my fridge and pantry. I'd get on my feet soon, anyway, so there was no point in making a big deal out of it.

Living in New York wasn't cheap, but I wouldn't trade it for anything. If there was ever a city that understood my own particular brand of chaos, it was here. With so many people choking the streets at every hour of the day, I couldn't help but blend in, no matter how much of a mess I was or if my shoes didn't match.

I enjoyed my commute, even on the days when I was running so far behind schedule that I knew I was going to get reamed out when I got there.

The office I worked in was bare-bones, to put it delicately. Our desks were particle board with peeling coats of gray paint. The walls were thin and let in almost every possible sound from the traffic outside. Many of our computers were still the old bulky kind where the monitor weighed about thirty pounds and was the size of an overfed toddler. Print journalism was dying an ugly death, and my workplace made no secret of it. The only people left in the business were the ones too stupid to smell the roses or the ones who enjoyed it too much to care. I liked to think I was a little bit of both.

As soon as I arrived, Hank came storming out from his corner office—a desk just like the rest of ours, except his was tucked in the corner of the large space we all shared. He was our lead editor, and pretty much the only person I ever directly dealt with.

There was, of course, Mr. Weinstead, but he didn't bother with the grunt-work. He just made sure we had advertisers for our magazine and that somebody paid the rent for our little slice of the skyscraper we called an office.

My best friend, Candace, was waving her arms and bulging her eyes at me from her desk as Hank approached. I gathered that she was trying to warn me, but wasn't sure what it was she thought I could do if Hank was about to lay another dumpster assignment on me.

Hank sized me up, as he had a habit of doing. He had thick eyebrows that looked disturbingly similar to his mustache, which also had the confusing effect of making it look like he had a third eyebrow above his lip, or maybe two mustaches over his eyes. I could never decide which. He was gray at the temples but still had all the nervous energy of a young man.

"On time today?" he barked. It was almost an accusation, like he was trying to figure out what my angle was.

"Yes?" I tried.

"Good. Maybe I won't fire you quite yet."

"You've been threatening to fire me since I started working here. What's that, three years now? Just admit it, Hank. You couldn't bear the thought of losing me or my talent."

Candace, who was listening in from her desk, stuck her finger in her mouth and mocked gagging. I tried not to grin back at her, because I knew Hank sniffed out fun like a bloodhound and would do whatever it took to squash it.

Hank lowered his mustaches—or eyebrows—in annoyance. "The only thing I'll admit is I enjoy having someone to dump the assignments no one else will take on. Speaking of which..."

"Wild guess. You're going to have me interview the owner of a garbage hauling company. No, wait. Maybe it'll be the guy who owns that business where they pick up dog poop from in front of your house for a low monthly fee. Am I close?"

"No," growled Hank. "You're going to pose as an intern at Galleon Enterprises. They're a—"

"Hotshot marketing business. Yeah," I said. "I know. You may keep my nose buried in crap, but believe it or not, I do actually stay up to date with the business world." I said it with a hint of pride. It was true, after all. Everybody here could make me into a joke or a laughing stock, and sometimes it was even easier to play along. But at the end of the day, I was a journalist, and I took my job seriously. I read editorials, I kept apprised on stock market performance to sniff up-and-comers in the business world, and I even read several blogs about journalism and writing to keep sharp.

"You're going to do whatever it takes to gather dirt on Bruce Chamberson."

"What kind of dirt?" I asked.

"If I knew that, do you think I'd be sending you in there?"

"Hank... This sounds suspiciously like a *good* assignment. Am I missing a punchline somewhere?"

For once, the hard expression on his face softened, even if it was just a touch. "I'm giving you a chance to prove you're not a fuck up. I expect you to fail miserably, for the record."

I set my jaw. "I won't let you down."

He looked at me like an idiot for a few seconds until I realized he had just said he expected me to fail.

"You know what I meant," I groaned before heading to Candace's desk.

She leaned forward, smiling wide. Candace was somewhere around my age. Twenty-five, maybe a little younger. I met her two years ago when I started working for Hank and *Business Insights* magazine. She had boyishly short blonde hair, but a cute enough face to pull it off and huge blue eyes. "Galleon Enterprises?" she asked. "They're a fortune 500 company, you know."

"Do you think it would be okay if I peed my pants now, or should I maybe wait until no one's watching?" I asked.

Candace shrugged. "If you pee on Jackson's desk, I'll cover for you. I think he has been stealing my yogurts out of the fridge."

"I'm not your biological weapon, Candace."

"Galleon Enterprises," she mused, almost wistfully. "You *have* seen pictures of the CEO, Bruce Chamberson and his brother, right?"

"Should I have?"

"Only if you're into gorgeous twins with a side of melted panties."

"Okay. Ew. I think if hot guys are melting your panties, you may want to get that checked out."

"All I'm saying is, don't tell me I didn't warn you to buy some thermal panties before your first day."

I squinted. "Please tell me that's not really a thing."

She jutted her head forward, mouth open in a *duh* kind of way. "Come on, Nat. What do you think female astronauts wear?"

As usual, I was left feeling dazed, confused, and a little disturbed after my conversation with Candace. I enjoyed her, though. I didn't have time for friends in the traditional sense— the kind of way sitcoms made you think everybody with a pulse lived their lives. Watch a few TV shows and you'd think the average adult spent ninety to ninety-five percent of their lives just hanging out with friends or working. Not to mention how the whole "working" part was also just a different backdrop to hanging out with friends.

Maybe it was just me, but my life was more like five percent friends, sixty percent work, and thirty-five percent worrying about work. Oh, and ten percent sleeping. Yes, I know that's more than one hundred percent, and no, I don't care. The point is that my life was no sitcom. It was a whole lot of lonely with a healthy dose of fear that I'd end up homeless, or worse, forced to move somewhere else and give up on my dream. And worse than all of that was the looming possibility that I was going to become Braeden. I'd end up in my old room with silly-putty stains on the walls from where my *One Direction* and *Twilight* posters used to hang.

Candace was a small dose of the life I wanted, and she was one I wished I had more time for, so I happily took the lasting feeling of confusion I was always left with after speaking to her.

Once I was back at my desk, the reality of my assignment started to sink in. Candace could make it into a joke if she wanted, but after two years, I was finally getting a chance to prove myself. I *could* write an amazing story. I could prove I deserved the better jobs—the higher paying jobs. For once, I wasn't going to mess it up.

2

BRUCE

There's a place for everything, and everything has its place. They were words to live by. My mantra.

I started my morning at exactly five thirty. No snooze button. I took a five-mile jog, spent exactly twenty minutes at the gym, and then rode the elevator back up to the penthouse for a cold shower. Breakfast was two whole eggs, three egg whites, a bowl of oatmeal, and a handful of almonds to eat separately when I was finished. I had set out my clothes for work the night before. Black, custom-tailored suit with a gray shirt and a red tie.

I liked order. I liked structure. It was the principle behind my business model and one of the primary factors that led to my success. Achievement was a two-part formula as simple as identifying the steps required to reach a goal and then taking those steps. Almost anyone could identify the steps, but not many had the self-discipline and control to follow them down to the letter.

I did.

I went through a nasty, complicated break up just three months ago, and lately, it had felt even easier to focus on the routine. Maybe I was getting more dependent on it by the day, but frankly, I didn't care. I'd happily bury myself in work if it meant forgetting. I'd push anyone and everyone away if it meant I didn't need to feel that sting again.

I had my driver pick me up at exactly seven in the morning to take me to the office. I worked out of an eighteen story building downtown. My twin brother and I bought it five years ago, floor by floor. Our first goal had been to operate out of New York. That took us a year. Our next was to rent a space in what used to be the Greenridge building, a modern, granite and glass monolith in the center of downtown. That took two months. Eventually, we wanted to own the whole thing. That took five years.

But here we were.

I pulled out my phone and dialed my brother, William. He answered, voice thick with sleepiness. "The fuck?" he groaned.

I felt my pulse quicken. We might look the same, but our personalities couldn't have been more different. William slept with a different woman every week. He perpetually overslept and missed work. He'd show up with lipstick smears on his neck and earlobes or with his shirt untucked. If he was anyone else, I would have fired him the moment I met him.

Unfortunately, he was my brother. Also unfortunately, he had my same sense for business, and despite his lack of professionalism, he was critical to Galleon Enterprises.

"I need you here," I said. "We're screening the interns today for the publicity piece."

There was a long pause. Long enough to tell me he had no idea what I was talking about.

"The interns. The ones you suggested we bring in? The ones who are going to soak up everything we show them and 'spew our diamond-crusted garbage to the media.' I assume you don't remember saying any of that?"

William groaned, and I thought I heard the soft voice of a woman in the background. "Right now, no. I don't remember that. Once I've injected a metric fuck-ton of caffeine into my veins, then yeah, maybe it'll start ringing a bell."

"Just get here. I'm not going to spend all morning interviewing your interns."

IT WAS ALMOST LUNCH, AND I'D SPENT ALL MORNING INTERVIEWING interns. I checked my watch. It was the kind of watch Navy SEALs wore, which meant I could dive up to a hundred and twenty-five meters with it on. I wasn't sure when I might need the ability to spontaneously go for an ocean dive, but I'd always found a satisfying comfort from knowing I was prepared for every last thing life could throw at me. I kept two extra sets of clothes in my office and in my driver's car at all times, business and casual. I had worked with a nutritionist to make sure my food intake was as optimally balanced as possible to keep me from feeling any energy dip or lethargy during my workday. I even had an extra phone with all my contacts and information backed up in case something happened to mine unexpectedly.

Every possibility was covered. No surprises. No setbacks. Most importantly, I never made the same mistake twice. *Never.*

One of the newest additions to my policy on avoiding repeat mistakes had been staying out of relationships. It wasn't worth it.

I could leave behind the more complicated pursuits like women and commitments for the simple ones. Speaking of which, there was a banana with my name on it—literally—in the break room. I could've kept it in my desk, of course, but I preferred the excuse to get up and take a walk a little while before lunch. It also meant I had a chance to interact with my employees. Talking with employees usually just meant listening to them kiss my ass, but I knew it was good for morale to mingle from time to time. People worked better for someone they liked.

I thanked the sixth intern I had interviewed that morning and stood to show her out of my office. Like the interns before her, she had been fresh out of college, wide-eyed, and terrified. I hadn't expected much else, but I wasn't sure how William expected to screen the candidates. He wanted someone who would absorb everything we did in the most favorable light possible, because he was going to set up a series of interviews with the media once they had learned enough. He said it would be free PR right before we launched our newest branch in Pittsburg.

One advertising philosophy we took very seriously was the idea of coming from as many angles as possible. We didn't just want our clients to dump all their money into radio or TV commercials. We got creative, and turning interns into our own relatively free advertising was just another facet of our strategy. It wasn't as much about the money as it was about playing the game, and we both loved the challenge. Think differently. Act faster. Take bigger risks. It was also another opportunity for potential clients to see the innovative and creative ways we used to market our own business. After all, if you want the best clients to pay *you* to market for *them,* you damn well better market yourself like a pro.

William and I had always played off each other's personalities well. He pushed me to take more risks than I would with the business, and I helped reign him in when he was too reckless.

I pushed my chair back in at my desk and drained the last of my water.

My stomach gurgled at the thought of the banana I had waiting for me. My diet had very little sugar in it, and over time, bananas had come to be the highlight of my culinary life. I knew it was ridiculous, which was why I would never admit it to anyone. But the banana I had before lunch was often the best part of my day. William said the employees who were afraid of me had learned to stay out of the break room if the banana was still there. The ones who were looking to kiss my ass would wait around it like it was bait.

The office was clean and modern in design. William and I paid an interior designer to put the look together and spared no expense. Having a clean, pleasing design was more than a luxury, it was a business model. We didn't just want our competition to think we were top of the line in every respect, we wanted our employees to feel it too. People worked differently when they thought they were at the top and wanted to stay there.

The break room was a glass rectangle overlooking an indoor courtyard area covered in just about every flower we could find that would survive indoors.

Each floor of the building had about eighty employees working at any given time, and I always had been quick to remember faces and names.

So when I didn't recognize the girl wearing a navy pencil-skirt and white blouse, I knew she was one of the interns. Her hair was pulled into a ponytail and she had missed a lock of hair that was catching the air from the overhead vent, flapping lazily and drawing my eye. She was pretty, with expressive, hazel eyes, a mouth that looked accustomed to mischievous grins and quick turns of phrase, and a body that she clearly took care of.

None of that mattered though. What mattered was the object in her hand.

The half-eaten object in her hand with my name written on it in sharpie. Only the neatly written "BRU" was visible before the peeled back flaps of the banana obscured the rest.

There were four other people in the break room, all of whom saw what was in her hand and had moved themselves to the farthest corners of the room. They were watching her like she was holding a grenade with the pin pulled, all while making efforts to casually slip out of the room before the explosion they knew was about to come.

The girl noticed me then.

Her eyes widened slightly and she sucked in a gasp, which seemed to lodge part of the banana in her throat. She started coughing and half-choking.

I saw red. She must be an intern, and she had the fucking nerve to touch my banana? To *eat* it? So when I moved to her side and slapped her back to help her dislodge whatever was stuck in her throat, I patted her with a little more force than I intended.

She grunted, coughed, and swallowed. Her cheeks ignited with a splotchy red as she looked me up and down, plopping herself in a chair by the large table at the center of the room to catch her breath.

"Do you know who I am?" I asked once she seemed to be fully recovered from choking on my banana. My throat was tight with rage and indignation. She was a small injection of chaos into my life, a sabotage of my routine. All my natural impulses were practically screaming for me to eliminate her from my life as fast as possible like a healthy body would attack a virus.

"You're Bruce Chamberson," she said.

The half-eaten banana was sitting beside her. I drew her attention to my finger before flicking the peel over the banana so she could read the full name written on the side.

Her mouth fell open. "I'm so, so sorry, Mr. Chamberson. I just forgot my lunch and I didn't see your name when I grabbed it. I thought it was complimentary, or—"

"A complimentary banana?" I asked dryly. "You thought Galleon Enterprises supplied its employees with a single, solitary banana?"

She paused, swallowed, and then shook her head. "Oh God," she said, sinking into her chair like all the air was seeping out of her. "Something tells me I'm not going to get the internship after this."

"Something tells you wrong. You're hired. Your first job every day will be to buy me a banana and bring it to my office, no later than 10:30." I made sure not to let surprise touch my features, even though it was spiking through me. *What the fuck was I doing?* She was attractive, and not in the way I could just notice off-handedly. She made something stir up inside me. I hadn't felt any ounce of sexual desire since I ended things with Valerie, but this intern was quickly changing that. I didn't just feel a curiosity about how good she'd look with that skirt hiked up to her hips, I wanted to know if she was quiet or loud in bed, if she'd dig her fingernails into my back or if she would lay herself out for me like a prize to be claimed. Yet at the same time, I wanted to eject her from my life as fast as humanly possible. She was everything I'd been trying to avoid. Everything I didn't want.

Her eyebrows drew down in confusion. "I'm hired?" she asked.

I pushed down all my doubts. I told her she was hired in front of everyone in the break room, and I wasn't about to look like I'd lost my shit in front of them. I had to own it. "Don't look so pleased with yourself. If I liked you, I would send you packing. You're going to wish you never touched my banana, Intern. I promise you that."

3

NATASHA

I let the water run over me in the shower, not caring that it was hot enough to sting. It was something to distract me from my latest blunder, which might well be the biggest of my life. I wanted to prove myself to Hank so badly, and now I wasn't sure how I was ever going to even get a sniff of anything juicy on Bruce Chamberson. Getting hired in the first place *was* admittedly a big hurdle I hadn't been sure I'd overcome, but the way it happened couldn't have gone any worse.

The worst part was how hard it had been to keep from breaking into immature giggles every time he talked about "his banana." It was beyond ridiculous. The guy looked like a super-model with ice for blood. His eyebrows seemed naturally drawn, eyes slightly narrowed at all times, like he hoped he could glare hard enough to make you evaporate into a cloud of vapor. My knees nearly buckled when he walked into the break room. I had done my due diligence as far as google stalking went, of course, but pictures didn't do him justice. He was *tall* in the perfect kind of way. Not lanky and almost freakishly like an NBA player, but with perfect proportions and a larger-than-life, ultra-masculine kind of way. He had just enough muscle to show through his neatly tailored suit. I hadn't looked into his brother yet, but they were supposedly twins, as hard as that was to believe. I hadn't been asked to gather dirt on William Chamberson, just Bruce. William was a bridge I'd cross when I got there.

But Bruce... He was a bridge I wasn't sure I wanted to get off, no matter how much it felt like it might twist at any moment and send me plunging to my death.

And his face. *God.* If he hadn't been so busy glaring a hole straight through me, I probably would've just spilled into a hot mess of a puddle at his feet. My survival instinct was the only thing that kept my mouth working. He had a jawline sharp enough to cut yourself on, eyes like blue, burning coals, and a mouth far too sensual and kissable for someone who seemed so stiff.

He was like an angry robot. Amendment. An angry *sex* robot. The kind that looked so good you didn't care if it only beeped and buzzed at you.

I let out a long, dramatic sigh and rinsed the last of the conditioner from my hair before drying off and starting my routine to get ready. I needed to be on time. It was my first day at Galleon Enterprises, and something in my gut told me there was no room for mistakes or tardiness with a man like Bruce Chamberson. But I couldn't stop thinking about the glint of life in his eyes when he told me I'd regret ever touching his banana. He was joking with me, even as he threatened me, and I couldn't reconcile that fact with the idea that he was an emotionless robot, no matter how hard I tried.

There was more to him than meets the eye, that much was for certain.

I WAS LATE. I'D DONE EVERYTHING IN MY POWER TO BE ON TIME, including planning on catching the train that should've had me at Galleon with thirty minutes to spare. I'd even shooed Braeden out of my apartment the night before and texted my parents to help ensure he wouldn't end up back at my place in a few hours. Of course, I *hadn't* budgeted time for the explosive diarrhea my French bulldog, Charlie, decided to have all over the apartment. He was a nervous pooper, and he was also extremely empathetic. I guess he picked up on my nerves and cluster-bombed the apartment as a kind of canine act of solidarity.

When I came out of the elevator on the top floor of Galleon, I was seven minutes late. By my standards, it wasn't that bad. Bruce was standing outside the elevator with a furious look on his face that told me his standards were more precise than my own.

"You're late," he said. His voice was flat, emotionless.

"I'm sorry, my dog—"

"I'm not interested in your excuses. The time will be docked from your pay."

I raised an eyebrow. "I'm an intern. I'm not getting paid."

His jaw clenched and his eyes narrowed.

Whoops. Somebody doesn't like being corrected.

"My office. Now."

He stormed off, leaving me no choice but to follow him with a sinking feeling in my stomach. My stupid mouth got me into hot water with Bruce when I ate his banana, and from the looks of his rigid posture and quick pace, my mouth wasn't done writing checks it couldn't cash. An ill-advised, dirty little seed of fantasy had been planted in my brain sometime between the banana and this morning, and I kept having to suppress images of Bruce locking me in his office so he could bend me over his knee and spank me. It was ridiculous. I wasn't even into that kind of stuff. Granted, if you played the game of describing my solitary sexual experience with a movie title, you'd win by picking *Fast and Furious*. Although, it'd fit better if the movie had been called *Fast and Underwhelming*, but I doubted anyone in Hollywood would greenlight that.

I fought the urge to put my hands up to shield my eyes as I

was led through his office. I was pulled over once for speeding when I used to drive, and I remember the feeling of mortification as people passed by, peeking in my window with gloating expressions. *Glad it was you, sucker*, was written all over their faces back then, just like it was now.

This was worse. A lot worse. It wasn't just my pride being dragged through the mud as I trailed behind Bruce like a sad, scolded puppy. It was the potential of impressing Hank. Everybody here was a possible source, and the more they saw me as a joke, the less likely I would be to learn anything useful from them.

Assuming I wasn't fired, I was going to be working here for the next few weeks. Months, even. However long it took to find dirt on Bruce. And frankly, I was getting hungrier for dirt by the minute. I didn't just want to know if he was the captain of a corrupt ship, though. I wanted to know why he was trying so hard to convince everybody he had the personality of a wet blanket. I also wanted to know why anyone at *Business Insights* even suspected Bruce was up to something suspicious. He certainly didn't seem to fit the mold of the shady businessman at first glance.

He closed the door to his office and walked to the blinds, pulling the string so we were completely alone.

"I don't need to remind you how important it is to be on time, correct?" he asked, leaving me to stand as he moved to his desk and started pulling out a small box, envelopes, and a piece of paper that he set on his desk in front of me.

Oh, God. This is the part in my fantasy where he pulls out a whip, and I tell him I'm not into all that kind of jazz, but he bends me over anyway. And he tells me I've been a naughty, naughty girl.

I squeezed my eyes shut, wishing I could stop being an idiot for just a fraction of a second for once. "Very important," I gulped. "It won't happen again. Probably. You never know when lightning will strike, and all that. But I'll try my hardest to be on time every day from now on."

"Yes. You will. Because I'm going to make something abundantly clear to you, Natasha Flores."

I ignored the way my skin prickled with warmth to hear him say my name. I guessed he had looked at the resume I submitted, because my name never came up during the banana incident or afterwards.

"I am not a nice man. You're not here because I want to become friends with you, or to fuck you," he added casually, as if it was a perfectly reasonable assumption he needed to clear off the table. "You're here because I don't like you, and I'm going to enjoy making you quit."

"I can really be charming if you give me a chance," I said through a throat so tight I was surprised my voice wasn't a shrill whistle. Even though he just explicitly said he *wasn't* trying to sleep with me, hearing the idea come out of his mouth seemed to make the fantasy bouncing around in my head grow even more clear. It wasn't a romantic fantasy. It was purely physical, and I would've challenged any woman to not look at Bruce Chamberson without having some ill-advised thoughts. It meant nothing. It was just chemicals and hormones.

He looked me up and down, eyes not lingering in any of the places they were supposed to. "Tell me then, Intern. How exactly do you plan to charm me? Is it with your work ethic? Your tendency to take things that belong to other people and put them in your mouth? Or is it that you think you'll seduce me?"

I straightened. I couldn't pin him down. One minute, I thought he was cold and empty on the inside. The next, I was absolutely sure he was teasing me. What was more, I was sure he was enjoying it.

"I didn't realize robots had the capacity to be seduced," I said. "You're sure there's not just a lever I can pull in your back-panel?"

There was nothing robotic in the glare he fixed on me. I

regretted talking back immediately, but there was no taking away my words. They hung in the silence between us, dangling there for me to watch with cringing helplessness.

"You are an aberration," he said simply, ignoring my jab. "My ability to deal with aberrations is part of what makes me so good at my job."

"I find that offensive. *I think.*"

"Good. You were supposed to. *Now,*" he said sharply, as if our discussion had come to a neat and orderly resolution. "This is your work phone." He handed me a cell phone that appeared to already be set up. "Your password is 'BANANA,' and no, you can't change it. That phone is as much mine as it is yours, so think carefully if you plan to use it for any sexting."

He was messing with me now. I knew he was. Every time I started to really think there was nothing in that gorgeous head of his except whirring machinery and circuits, he let a little humanity seep through, and I absolutely hated how interested it was making me. I was a journalist, after all, and I wasn't sure I had encountered a mystery quite as compelling as Bruce Chamberson. My leading theory? He was actually a normal guy, but he held himself back around everyone. I just needed to find out if the real Bruce only slipped out when he was around me, or if he was bad at holding it in around everyone.

"And these?" I asked, pointing to the envelopes and the paper.

He flipped open the flap on one of the envelopes to show me a laminated bag full of credit cards, some sort of instruction manual, and a set of car keys. The other bag contained a passport that somehow had my face on it, even though I definitely hadn't ever gotten myself a passport.

"These are some of the tools you'll need to perform your duties as my intern. Keys to the company car, which you'll use to act as my personal driver. Credit cards for business functions, dinners with clients, or outings sponsored by Galleon. You'll be required to attend all of those, by the way. And the phone is so I can reach you at any hour, day or night. You'll always have it on. I'm the only one with the number. It's my direct line to you."

I felt my nostrils flare, which only happened when I was the kind of mad where you start thinking about your forehead as a weapon instead of just the inside of your palm. Being sexy as sin didn't give him a license to treat me like a slave. "You realize the normal duties for an intern are more like running copies, sitting in on meetings, or making coffee runs for everyone, right?" I had to clamp my mouth shut from saying I did have another job. Technically, I did. I'd need time to write down and organize anything I learned here and prepare it for the piece I'd eventually write. From the sounds of things, he didn't plan on giving me any free time, which wasn't going to make my life easy.

"I don't care what's normal. I never have. This is an exceptional company run by exceptional people. If you are going to be part of it in any capacity, I expect you to work as tirelessly as the rest of us."

"Let me guess. The fact that I'm still not getting paid has no bearing on any of these superhuman expectations, right?"

"Good. You're learning. Maybe there's some hope for you, after all."

4

BRUCE

The intern's first day was an exercise in self-control for me. Every impulse in my body was screaming to get rid of her. She was a walking disaster. She spilled coffee on my shirt, which forced me to use one of my spare outfits. Frankly, I wasn't even confident that a single spare outfit would be enough with this woman rampaging around in my life. She dented the company car when she was pulling it out of the parking garage because she swerved to avoid 'a huge grasshopper,' even though I'd lived in New York City for most of my life and never once seen a grasshopper. To top it all off, the banana she brought for me wasn't ripe enough.

It wasn't even lunch yet, and the intern had introduced more chaos into my life than I'd experienced in the past year. My blood pressure was spiked and I was seriously starting to question my motives for keeping her around.

I *was* attracted to her, against all reason. She had chestnut brown hair that complimented those hazel eyes and tanned skin of hers. She also had a way of dipping her chin toward her chest when I was reaming her out, which made her big eyes seem even bigger and full of mischief as she was forced to look up at me.

Her lips would curve up on one side, like pissing me off actually amused *her*.

The fucking woman was going to make me lose my mind.

"You, uh... Good?"

I spun, ready to throat-punch whoever had just walked into the break room. I was still clutching the banana peel that was more green than yellow. It was my brother.

I sighed. William was the last person I wanted to talk to when I was feeling on edge. I didn't even want to *see* him. He had a way of wearing his hair in a kind of perpetual mess and keeping a few days' stubble on his face. He rarely wore a tie, choosing to leave a couple buttons undone so he could more easily scout out women who were hungry enough to be his next one-night-stand.

Looking at him made me itch for a comb. He was my mirror image, except he was what I might've been if I didn't have obsessive-compulsive tendencies with a heavy dose of perfectionism. He was me without control. The definition of a loose cannon. Most of all, he was what I could've been if Valerie had never happened. Minus the ridiculously messy hair, at least.

I threw the banana peel in the trash. "Yes. I'm, 'uh' good."

He crossed his arms, watching me with a twinkle of amusement in his eyes. "Then why does it look like someone just took a shit in your banana pudding? And since when do you eat anything but perfectly yellow bananas? That one looked more like a cucumber."

"Since the intern from hell arrived." Figuring she could find a suitable banana had been a mistake, and it wasn't one I'd repeat.

"I assume it's a stupid question to ask why you don't fire her?"

"You assume correctly. I can't fire her. Not yet."

"I see." William scrunched his forehead up skeptically. "So she's hot?"

I gave him a suffering look. "Really? You do realize we only *look* identical, right? One of us is able to keep his cock in his pants, especially at work."

"Hey, I'm not the one taking my cock out of my pants at work. Those women were very persistent. Besides, I know you aren't opposed to getting your dick wet. There was that one woman... Shit, what was her name?"

"Valerie." I tried not to grate her name out. Maybe there had been something close to real feelings for her inside me once. Now, I just felt an empty sense of loss, not because she was gone but because I'd given up part of myself I wish I could have back.

"Right," said William. "What a raging bitch. You know, I once thought about framing her for some kind of petty crime as your birthday present? Nothing too serious, obviously, but I thought a couple nights in jail would be good for her."

"Please tell me you're joking."

"Yeah, totally joking," he said in a way that told me he wasn't.

"I gotta say. I hated her *before* she cheated on you. Imagine how I feel about her now, right?" he grinned, punching my shoulder like it was all a good joke. "And then there was that phase you went through with the whole secretary thing. Remember?" He asked, his face split with a grin. "I swear, you would only fuck women if they had to wear pantsuits and pencil skirts to work. I was starting to think you had a fetish."

I took a deep, controlled breath in through my nose. William always managed to make just about any conversation about sex, and he never had any problem talking about my sex life.

"Yes, I have been in relationships. And no, I don't have a fetish."

With what I had already diagnosed as chronically bad timing, the intern came stumbling into the room. Literally. Her heel caught on the carpet and she nearly spilled coffee on me again.

William raised his eyebrows at her, scanning her body and no doubt taking in her pencil skirt. He grinned. "Speaking of fetishes..."

Natasha looked up at William and nearly spilled the coffee again. She looked to me again, then to William, confusion written all over her face. She must've known I had a twin though, because a look of realization settled over her more quickly than it did on most people who saw us together for the first time.

"Twins," said William. He stepped closer to her, putting a hand on the small of her back as if she needed to be steadied. To be fair, I guess, she probably did. From the little I knew of the intern, she likely fell on her face without warning from time to time.

"So you're the polite one," she said to William. "I guess that makes you the evil twin, Bruce?"

William smirked at that. "Hey. Can we keep her? I like her already. No wonder you've got a hard-on for her."

"I'm the one without STDs," I growled, ignoring him as much as I could.

William put his hands up, which thankfully meant he wasn't groping her anymore. "Easy there, killer. I always use protection. I'm clean as a whistle."

"Thanks," I said roughly, snatching the coffee from her hand and hoping she'd leave. I didn't want my brother to have any more chances to try to fuck her. Because she had a pulse, she was pretty, and most importantly, he suspected I wanted her for myself. In William's recipe book, that was as close to an aphrodisiac as mother nature could ever hope to provide.

The intern stayed put, still looking between us like she expected us to reveal it had been an optical illusion all along. "It's uncanny," she said.

"Not really. It's genetics," I said.

"Ignore him." William followed her to the fridge as she rummaged for God-knew-what. "He has a chronic condition. They found the stick up his ass when we were just kids and the doctors said we couldn't remove it without killing him. Naturally, we all tried as hard as we could to pull it out, but the stubborn bastard never gave us an inch. See, he's a tight-ass, too. It's tragic, really, when you think about it. Sometimes I lay awake at night trying to figure out which came first... The stick, or the tight ass."

The intern was trying to cover a smile by ducking her head behind the refrigerator door, but I could hear her choppy breaths as she bit down laughter.

"Out," I said to William.

He took a step toward the door as if he'd been planning on leaving anyway. "By the way. Keep wearing the pencil skirts. The whole secretary look. It's like a fetish for him. Really gets him excited. He's like an old car. Hard to start up, but once you get him going he *really* goes. Just keep at it, kid."

She looked down, smoothing the ruffles from her skirt, cheeks burning red. How many hours had I known her and how many times had she already blushed? I'd never admitted it to a living soul, but it was possible that I did have a little bit of a preference for the secretary look. I also might have always enjoyed women who blush easily.

None of that was important, though, because the list of things I did not enjoy about the woman was so long. She was the disaster to my perfection, the wrecking ball that would smash through every carefully built wall and comfort I'd spent my life building up. She was absolutely one hundred percent wrong for me in almost every sense of the word, and yet I still didn't fire her. I knew I wouldn't, either. I'd keep her on until...

Until what?

I spent the rest of the afternoon wondering what exactly it was. What the hell was I waiting for?

I WAS SITTING AT A TABLE IN SEASONS 12 LATER THAT EVENING. IT was a white tablecloth, candles, and jackets and ties type of place. There was a huge fish tank in the center of the dining room filled with exotic, expensive breeds, including a shark and a large moray eel that kept peeking out from a cluster of rocks, mouth flapping soundlessly as it seemed to taste the water. I absently wondered if the captivity ever made fish go crazy as I watched the eel. Humans would lose their mind in a box like that in a matter of weeks, maybe days.

I thought about how Natasha had called me a robot. Maybe she wasn't entirely wrong, at least in some respects. It wasn't that I didn't feel or crave all the things most people did. The difference was that I'd learned to suppress it all. I'd *trained* myself to. I guess William and I each had our own defense mechanisms for the shit we grew up in the middle of. He taught himself not to care about anything. I taught myself to wrestle control even from the most uncontrollable situations. I learned to take chaos and make order.

It hadn't all happened at once. Life had thrown most of what it could at me, and bit by bit, I'd shut myself off. I guess the problem was that burying the things you want to protect will keep them safe, but it also keeps them out of reach. Somewhere along the way, I think I had walled away too much of myself and ended up with nothing to show the world except professional competence and a face women liked to look at. I could almost laugh. Natasha had known me all of two days and seemed to already have hit the nail on the head. I wasn't much better than a robot.

My mother and father arrived ten minutes late. My mother was in her fifties. William and I had her eyes and eyebrows, while we had my father's square jaw and broad shoulders. God knew where we got our height, though, because both my parents were a few inches shy of six feet.

My father had a way of walking that managed to disrespect any environment with a sort of casual ease you couldn't teach. It was something between a waddle and a swagger, with a constantly swiveling head and a sour smirk on his lips. He looked at the world like he was unimpressed, even though the most impressive thing he had ever done was bring William and me into the world. He seemed to think so too, which was why we had to endure monthly "get-togethers" which were little more than thinly veiled money grabs.

Agreeing to even meet them at this point was the last shred of respect I showed them for raising me. I'd more than paid any debts I could've possibly owed them, but I couldn't quite bring myself to cut them off completely. Not yet, at least.

My mother was an unassuming woman. Frail with a permanently surprised look on her face and an inability to evenly apply her lipstick, which always made her upper lip look lopsided.

"Where's your brother?" asked my father as he sat himself down.

"He couldn't make it." Actually, I had told William to meet me at a restaurant on the other side of the city. He was probably figuring out I misled him by now, but he'd get over it. The dumbass was always giving our parents money instead of realizing it just made things worse.

My mother looked nervously to my father. She knew their chances of getting money out of me were about as good as squeezing water from a rock.

"Son," said my father. He leaned back and flicked his tongue across his lips in a way that reminded me of a reptile. "We're not asking about a hand-out. We're looking for a business partner."

I didn't dignify that with a response. I let my eyes stay cold, my face expressionless.

He cleared his throat, doubling down on his nonchalance by spreading his arms across the back of my mother's chair and making a kind of "oh come on face." "It's pennies to you, Bruce. Fucking pennies. Did I raise you to be a selfish asshole, or was that your mother's fault?"

"I've more than paid my debt to you for raising me."

"Brucie," said my mother. "You don't owe us for raising you. You were our baby. We're just looking for some help since you're doing so well for yourself. Think about it. Your pocket change is our lottery ticket."

"A lottery ticket I've already given you two. Multiple times. And what do you have to show for it? Gambling losses, a boat you crashed because you were drunk off your asses, and all the plastic you've pumped into your faces? Money to pay off all the DUIs?"

They both stiffened at that. "You want to get on your high horse?" My father leaned in and planted his elbows on the table, lowering his voice slightly when his tone drew the eyes of nearby diners. "I'm not going to sit here and let you talk down to me. I changed your fucking diapers when you were shitting yourself, tough guy."

"Right," I said. "And now you want me to change yours? Take some of the money William and I have already given you and hire a nanny. I'm not your ATM."

I was surprised and more than a little relieved when they both got up and hurried out of the restaurant in a huff of indignation. They *did* have a breaking point, and I was happy to say I had become more and more able to find it quickly as the years had gone by. I could have refused their offers to meet all together, but the truth was I was waiting for something with them, too, just like with the intern. Trouble was, I didn't know what I was waiting for with them, either.

Maybe it was a side-effect of shutting myself down emotionally for so long. I couldn't even understand myself, anymore.

5

NATASHA

I woke up extra early to check in at *Business Insights*. Hank sat on his corner desk with crossed arms and those intimidating mustaches masquerading as eyebrows looming high on his forehead.

"So you're in?" he asked. "That's good. I'm actually impressed, Nat."

Pride swelled up in me. Hank had looked at me with pity for as long as I could remember. Maybe he did appreciate my writing, to some extent, but he had always treated me like a charity case. I was the one he felt too bad to cut loose. Hearing him say he was impressed felt like much-needed medicine, and I already craved more. I wanted to make him proud. I wanted to blow him away with an awesome story. "I'm in," I agreed.

"How'd you do it? Nail the interview?"

I made a *kinda-sorta* gesture by rocking my hand from side to side.

He gave me a confused look.

"All that matters is I got the job. Right?"

He chuckled. "Sure, Nat. Come to think of it, I don't think I want to know how you got the job. Knowing you, it probably involved a series of highly unlikely and borderline impossible coincidences."

I smiled, hoping he didn't see the red creeping into my cheeks. *Technically, it involved me putting his banana in my mouth.* "I wanted to warn you though. He wants me to work for him pretty much around the clock. I may not be able to check in too often."

Hank waved that off. "Then don't. All that matters is I have a story. I don't care if it takes you months to get it. You get dirt on him, and you'll get the payday of your life. Weinstead put a king's ransom on Bruce Chamberson's dirt, so we're going to get it."

"Weinstead wants it?" I asked. "What makes him want it so badly? And why is he so sure it's Bruce and not his brother? From what I've already learned, his brother seems like a much more likely suspect."

Hank shrugged. "Does it matter?"

That was Hank-eeze for "I don't know," which I knew better than to question. Hank was the big-wig, and he liked it that way. He didn't appreciate admitting when he wasn't in the loop on something.

I stopped by Candace's desk on my way out. She grinned knowingly. I had no idea what she thought it was she knew, but she was ready for me to spill it.

"Tell me everything," she said.

"There's nothing to tell. I interviewed. I got the job. Simple as that." I was stalling, and we both knew it. The truth was, I enjoyed teasing Candace. She was like a feisty little dog, and I enjoyed seeing her get riled up when I dangled something she wanted in front of her.

She folded her arms and fixed with me with a death glare. "Nat. I *know* you. Bullshit me and I'll kneecap you." She grabbed her umbrella and started taking little exploratory stabs at my knees, making me jump back, laughing.

"Jesus! Okay. *Okay!*" I said, having to grab the umbrella and rip it from her hands. I moved a little closer and lowered my

voice. "I ate Bruce Chamberson's banana. And not in the innuendo sense. Like a yellow banana that he wrote his name on with
Sharpie. Obviously, I didn't see his name on it or—" I trailed off at
the dumbfounded look on her face.

She watched me for a few seconds before she burst out laughing. "I'm sorry," she said. "It's just such a *you* thing to do. It's a
testament to your track record that I'm not even questioning if
you're joking with me. Of course, you ate his banana. I'm not
exactly making the connection here on how nibbling on his
banana got you a job, though."

"I'm trying to figure that one out, too."

"Did he like that you ate it or something? Maybe he's a perv.
Reading between the lines or something. You know?" She
lowered her voice in a horrible male impression. "Oh, Natasha.
I'm bananas for those lips. A little faster and I'll split.
Oh... oh..."

"Candace!" I hissed, grinning but looking around to make
sure no one was listening. "One, those were the worst puns I've
ever heard. Two, no. Just no. He's not like that. I mean, if he liked
it, he's a really good actor. It looked more like he wanted to rip my
head off and drop kick it out the window."

She raised her eyebrows and narrowed her eyes. "So he's kind
of barbaric? *Sexy.*"

"More like robotic. Sexy, yes, but he's like a microwaved
burrito. Scalding hot on the outside and cold as ice on the
inside."

"Please tell me you just compared a man to a burrito, because
I love that."

"I can confirm," I said, grinning.

She sighed. "Listen, Nat. I don't care if he's frozen on the
inside or not. You need to tap that. Forget the story. Forget everything. Something is going on there. You eat the guy's banana, he
hires you? Come on. There's your story. That is not an 'everything
is as it seems' scenario. Not by a long shot."

"I mean, he did pretty specifically say he wanted to hire me to punish me."

Candace spread her hands like I just confirmed her theory. "See? The guy is kinky as hell. He wants to take you to his sex dungeon or something. Think about it. You *need* to sleep with him to get him to open up. It's part of your job. It's goddamn journalistic integrity. You'd be in breach if you *don't* sleep with him."

I laughed, even though the ideas of Bruce and sex made my whole body throb with heat. At the same time, the thought of Bruce and a relationship made me feel cold on the inside. "I kind of hate him..." I said.

Candace blew a dismissive sound out of her mouth, knocking away a loose strand of her short-cropped hair. "You don't have to like him to sleep with him, you know. You're a big girl. Sometimes it's okay to just take it where you can get it. Sex doesn't have to be some big emotional statement, you know. It can just be fun."

I wasn't so sure about that, but I had to apologize and rush out of the building when I saw I was already on the verge of being late again. I forgot I had to drive now, so I wasn't dealing with the at least somewhat predictable subway system. I was dealing with New York traffic.

Bruce was waiting outside his building with a pissed off look on his face. I parked the now-dented company car and waited for him to get in. When he didn't move, I realized he actually expected me to get out and open the door for him.

Thirty minutes of traffic to travel three miles had me too annoyed to put up with his posturing, so I just reached over the passenger seat and pushed the door open.

He glared down at it, but eventually yanked it all the way open and got in the car.

"Isn't it kind of emasculating?" I asked. "Riding shotgun like this while your intern drives?"

He gave me a cold look. "No."

I cleared my throat a little uncomfortably and started driving. He had a way of answering my playful teases with so much hostility that I always kind of regretted it, but not completely. Messing with him was fun. Maybe it was just a natural impulse when somebody came off as so calm and in command. I wanted to see how he'd react if his feathers were ruffled. He was looking down at his phone and doing a pretty good job of pretending I didn't exist, which was going a long way toward debunking Candace's theory that he was actually interested in me.

"What are you up to over there?" I asked.

I felt him glaring at me from the corner of my eyes and decided to focus on the road instead of stare back into that icy heat. "I'm working."

"Oh," I said. "I thought I saw cat videos on your phone for a second."

"Do I look like someone who watches cat videos?"

I pressed my lips together. "I mean, who doesn't? Right?"

"I don't."

"I'll email you some today. Maybe a couple cute cats can soften you up a little."

He set his phone down in his lap and half-turned to face me. "Do you do it on purpose?"

"Do... what, on purpose?"

"Irritate me. Are you incapable of driving the car quietly while I get work done?"

"I figured the reason you forced me to be your little chauffeur was because you wanted the company."

"Yeah, well, you thought wrong."

I stole a look at him. He was focused on his phone again, but the amateur psychologist in me said his posture was a little defensive. Too stiff and rigid. "I see. Then why exactly am I acting as your driver again?"

"I want you to quit."

"Really?" I asked skeptically. "That sounds thin, even to me. I mean... First, your brother points out your fetish, and then you hire me for seemingly no reason. There's something else going—"

"Enough," he said quietly. "I don't have to explain myself to you. You work for me until you decide to quit. You do as I say until you decide to quit. It's really that simple. You don't have to understand it or like it. In fact, I hope you *don't* like it."

I pursed my lips but said nothing. Just as someone honked their horn, I could've sworn on my grandmother's grave I heard him mutter, *that will teach you to eat something that's not yours.*

I turned to look at him and nearly crashed into the car in front of me. There it was again. That spark of humanity underneath the machinery and wires under his perfect skin.

"Crashing the car and killing us *would* get you out of the job without technically quitting. But I don't think it's a good idea."

"If I didn't know better, I'd say you just tried to make a joke, Mr. Robot."

He gave me a dry look. "How about you drive the car instead of trying to figure me out."

"Is that what you think I'm doing? Trying to figure you out?" I made a *pfft* sound. "Don't flatter yourself."

"Great. I was worried you were going to start asking about the trauma of my childhood, or the horrible accident I had that led to my stunted personality."

"I'm not falling for it."

He shrugged. "That's fine."

"You *are* making that up, right?" I asked a few seconds later, hating that I couldn't resist taking his bait.

Infuriatingly, he just kept his head down as he typed up something on his phone. I thought I even saw the hint of a smirk on his lips. I quietly fumed the rest of the way to the office, and nearly put another dent in the car when I ramped up the curb and narrowly missed a street sign with the front fender. It had been a while since I drove a car, and despite what people seemed to believe, it wasn't at all like riding a bike. Then again, I had a long history of bike crashes, so maybe they weren't entirely wrong.

The first half of the workday went about the same as the previous day. I gathered coffee, no cream, and no sugar for Mr. Sex Robot. I had to go into three grocery stores to find a single banana that had no hints of green and no brown spots. I don't think I'd ever seen him as serious as he was when he was describing the specifications of the banana. At least ten inches. Firm. No bruises. No green. He even made me put my hands together so I had a way to measure the length and be sure it was big enough but not too big. It was more like he was telling me how to defuse a bomb in the basement of a kindergarten.

I came back just before lunch with the banana in hand and set it on his desk. He picked it up, turned it around, and made a ridiculous show of inspecting it. Finally, he nodded. "Hm. Not bad." Then he threw it in the trash and got up from his desk.

I pointed at the trash can, mouth open in shock. "Do you realize how many stores I had to go to for that stupid thing?"

"I can imagine. You were gone for an hour and ten minutes. Assuming you walked fast, that gave you time to go to three stores, maybe four if you found the produce sections quickly."

I rolled my eyes. "You're not helping the case with the whole robot thing. *Three stores, maybe four if...*" I said in my best robot impression but trailed off when I saw the look on his face.

"I'm precise," he said with a touch of defensiveness, which was new.

"Well, I'm just trying to figure out how you operate in the same world I do, where not everything goes perfectly. What happens if your train is late, or if you wake up sick one day?"

"I find a way to solve the problem. If I can't, I make a change to be sure I'm prepared and that I won't make the same mistake again."

He made me feel like a teenager, like I had to fight the urge to roll my eyes at everything he said. But I also felt like I was the victim of raging hormones that forced me to keep noticing the places where his dress shirt hugged his tight body in all the right places, and the way his legs looked in those slacks. *Sex robot,* I reminded myself. I might as well be getting turned on by a sports car. Yes, it was nice to look at, but there wasn't anything under the hood. Except what was probably a sculpted rack of abs and what I couldn't help assuming would be a fully functional, extra delicious *banana.*

There were hints of something about him. I wondered how much of the personality he was showing me was a defense mechanism, and how much was really him. But why was he hiding? *What* was he hiding? I guess it shouldn't have come as a surprise that my natural impulse was to head-butt my way straight through the walls he hid behind out of sheer curiosity. I also had a job to do. Maybe he was hiding the evil brain of a corrupt businessman behind those walls.

"So... You don't make the same mistakes twice? Is that why you have the personality of a washing machine? Did you get burned for being likable once?"

He paused mid-step, gave me a look I'd almost call startled, and then quickly smoothed his features back to neutral. "I was born this way."

"Right," I muttered, following after him as he headed to the break room. "So why exactly did you throw away the banana? Worried it was poisoned? Because I did consider it, but I settled for praying that you'd choke."

He stopped, half-turned his head to look at me, and if I didn't know better, I'd say he was fighting back an amused smile. "I threw it away because I already have a banana with my name on it waiting in the conference room. Unless, of course, some clueless intern is devouring it."

"Is that a common problem for you?" I asked.

"You're the only one who didn't see my name written in big-ass letters on the banana. So, no. It's not a common problem."

When we walked into the conference room, everyone stiffened at the sight of Bruce. It was easy to forget why I was really here, but at that moment, the reporter in me finally started to wake up a little. I needed to make an effort to find some time away from Bruce soon so I could try to squeeze information from his employees.

"Mr. Chamberson," said a woman in her thirties with a great body and a pretty face. There was an eagerness to her tone that had desperation written all over it. I folded my arms and watched in amusement from the doorway. *Stupid woman. Might as well throw yourself at a bag of potatoes.*

He gave her half of his attention while he reached for his banana, which I noted now had his name printed in large letters on every single surface so that no one could miss it anymore. He really did avoid making the same mistakes twice.

"Wait a second," I asked, interrupting the woman who was trying to explain some kind of glitch in the system that was slowing her department down. It sounded like a bogus story designed to get him to personally come to her desk, anyway. "You sent me on a wild banana hunt when you had one in here the whole time?"

He peeled open the banana and took a bite that I was *almost* positive wasn't meant to be seductive, but that only made it send warmth bubbling under my skin even more quickly. *He had such nice teeth. And those lips...*

"I had to make sure you were capable of getting me something more edible than the cucumber you brought me yesterday."

"It had a hint of green. If you thought that was a cucumber, you need your eyes checked."

I was conscious of everyone in the room staring at us with open astonishment. The only exception was the pretty woman, who was definitely giving me the territorial glare women had spent centuries perfecting. It was the glare that said, "you're sinking your claws into my scratching post, bitch, and if you don't back off, I'm going to claw your eyes out."

With effort, I ignored the attention and focused on Bruce. As much as I was tired of his attitude, there was something fun and exciting about trying to keep pace with him. Every word with him was part of some verbal sparring match I hadn't quite gotten my head around, but I found myself *wanting* to.

He took another bite of the banana, casually chewing as he watched me, and seemingly oblivious to the fact that the whole break room was staring. It was actually kind of cute how much he seemed to be enjoying his snack. There was a twinkle in his eyes as he chewed. It was the kind of look most people got when they were biting into a luxurious, calorie-packed dessert.

"We're having lunch with a pair of important clients. Have the car ready in ten minutes." He finished the last bite and tossed the peel toward the trash can without looking.

"You missed," I said as the peel caught the edge of the can and fell to the floor.

"Good thing I have an intern," he said over his shoulder.

I knelt down to pick up the peel in front of everybody, who watched me with a mixture of pity and cruel amusement. It was precisely at that moment when I decided this wasn't going to be a one-way battle. He wanted to make my life miserable? He wanted to force me to quit? Then I hoped he was ready for war, because I was going to show him I wasn't too scared to bite back.

THE RESTAURANT WAS FANCY. I GREW UP PRETTY CLOSE TO POOR, SO my line of distinction between a fancy restaurant and a normal one had always been whether shirt and shoes were required. Unfortunately, this place was at least a few notches above that, because even my business attire felt far too plain and cheap.

Everybody *looked* rich or important. It was practically dripping off them, from the glinting white teeth I would've needed sunglasses to look at directly to the weird quality I always felt rich people had in their skin. You are what you eat, and I guess rich people ate so much expensive food that even their skin started to look different.

Bruce had good skin too, I noticed. *For a robot.* I guess I shouldn't have been surprised. He was so infuriatingly organized that he probably had never touched his face with unwashed hands before, or had greasy fingers. It made me want to fling a french fry at him during lunch, but something told me this place didn't serve french fries, either. I was probably going to end up stabbing a duck liver with my fork while trying not to vomit for an hour.

We were seated in a corner booth a little separate from the rest of the lunch crowd. It wasn't busy, but every member of the staff still bustled around the room with a seeming urgency, as if the whole place was packed.

"Maybe your important business partners stood you up," I said once we sat.

"We're early. Fifteen minutes."

"Right," I said, as if I knew what that was like. One effect Bruce had on me already was forcing me into some semblance of a structured existence. I was still a walking disaster, but he was like a safety harness. Despite the way he could be stifling and obnoxiously distant, it was admittedly a little bit nice to feel like he was able to keep me from the worst of myself.

I still wanted him to realize he made a mistake when he decided to bully me. He wasn't going to fire me? Good. That meant I had free license to do whatever I wanted without worrying I was putting my real job on the line. And at the moment, what I wanted was a little payback.

His important clients showed up only a few minutes later.

They were a husband and wife team who were trying to set up some kind of expensive marketing plan for a new branch of their tech business, from what I gathered of their conversation. I'd spent my whole professional life trying to glean inside information on upcoming businesses from magazines and second-hand sources, so getting to sit at a table and have information fed directly to me was a rare treat.

Ultimately, they weren't talking about anything truly newsworthy. We were served drinks, and I helped myself to some of the wine, despite the warning glances Bruce kept shooting me. It seemed like he didn't want to chastise me in front of his clients, a point which I planned to take full advantage of. I ate crusty bread with crab dip while they talked about the dates they'd be rolling out the first big promotional push. I washed those down with a glass of wine.

We had some kind of green "reduction" from peas with edible flowers sprinkled in next. It looked pretty, and I was surprised to find it *tasted* pretty, too. Bruce was hardly touching any of his food, and he had only taken a few sips of his wine. He seemed much more focused on making sure the clients understood the business plan.

"...That will be on the seventeenth," said Bruce. "We'll run a few low budget campaigns to screen ad copy through the twenty-eighth of the following month. Once we have the top performers, we can start investing aggressively in the campaign. Just be sure you're prepared to deal with increased traffic on all your existing infrastructure, as well. Your new website isn't going to be the only part of your business benefiting from this. Remember, we're selling your brand."

The couple exchanged a look, nervous smiles on their faces. They liked what he was saying. They liked *how* he was saying it. I didn't blame them. Sitting in with Bruce made it clear how he had carved out one of the most powerful and influential clients. He spoke with so much passion and confidence about the marketing plan that it was impossible to doubt him. He looked like a man who had the world figured out, and maybe he did.

But, I thought with a mischievous twinge of excitement, I was one little slice of the world he hadn't figured out.

"Hmm," I said, taking another sip of my wine to try to look casual. It was probably a mistake, because my head was starting to spin already. "That would mean your main advertising campaign begins around two weeks before the launch of WeConnect." I waited for my words to sink in. Bruce had an easy time thinking of me as some kind of bumbling clutz, but I couldn't wait to see the look on his face when he realized I actually had a head on my shoulders.

Bruce looked like he was using every ounce of his self-control to keep from tearing my head off. It wasn't exactly the look I was hoping for, but it was satisfying in its own way.

"WeConnect?" asked the woman, saving me from Bruce for the moment.

The man nodded, eyes searching the table thoughtfully. "They're a startup. I've heard the name but don't remember the details."

"Every indication says they're going to be huge," I said. "They are completely crowd-funded and their Kickstarter already raised over thirty-five million. Basically, they think WeConnect is going to take everything Facebook, Instagram, and Twitter do and do all of it, but better. And you're talking about putting yourselves head-to-head with that."

They both looked to Bruce, who was staring at me. I tried not to wince for the inevitable explosion of his temper. Instead, he seemed like he was actually thinking about what I said. Finally, he nodded, slowly at first and then with more enthusiasm. "She's right. Damn. I don't know how we overlooked that."

I listened for the next half hour as Bruce came up with a plan to overcome the threat of WeConnect. I kept trying to squash the giddy feeling of pride and the way "she's right" kept replaying in my head. When I'd earned nothing but glares and incredulous looks from Bruce since starting my internship, the praise felt monumental. Just from a professional standpoint, of course. If I hoped to get any kind of inside information, I needed him to trust me.

I lost track of how many glasses I'd had of the wine sometime around the main course, which was lobster in the most simple but incredible butter sauce I'd ever tasted. I was working my way well past tipsy and into drunk territory. It had been my plan, originally, when he forced me out to lunch. I thought maybe if I was an embarrassment he'd stop trying to bully me into being his tag-along.

I was going to stop and do my best to sit quietly while the alcohol swirled around in my head. Impressing him had started to seem smarter than pissing him off, but I couldn't just snap my fingers and un-drunk myself.

The waiter moved to refill my glass, but Bruce put up a hand, stopping him with a subtle gesture. I had been about to stop him myself. Drunken me was offended that Bruce had the nerve to tell *me* when it was time to stop. Drunken me was also an idiot.

"Bring it on," I said, words slurring. I was further gone than I realized. I'd reached the point where the words out of my mouth were as much a surprise to me as to everyone else.

The waiter looked like he'd rather be anywhere at that moment. Bruce was still trying not to make a scene—trying to preserve his precious order in all things.

"Come on, big boy," I said. Somewhere, sober me was curled up in a ball deep inside my brain, cringing, because I knew that particular line wasn't one that was going to be easy to forget. Drunken me thought it was hilarious.

"She's had enough," he said, forcing the waiter to leave.

I slumped in my seat, looking defiantly at the couple, who now shifted and tried their hardest to look anywhere but at me. I couldn't make sense of much anymore. All I really wanted to do was lay down and go to sleep, but then I'd catch a glimpse of Bruce, who didn't need drunk goggles to look amazing. With the better part of a bottle of wine in me, he looked like some kind of shimmering angel. I felt something stupid and inappropriate boiling up in me and knew I was powerless to stop it.

There was a long, uncomfortable pause where everyone seemed to be waiting for something. I was too dizzy to even come close to figuring out what it was they expected. Of course, that didn't stop me from opening my mouth and saying the first thing on my mind.

"So, Brucie," I said. "Are you going to be the final course? Because I don't think I can share you with those two."

6

BRUCE

I apologized for the fifth time as I walked Donna and Gregory out to the valet. Natasha was slumped against my shoulder and I was half-carrying her out of the restaurant.

"It's okay, really. We were young once, too," said Donna.

Gregory just flashed a tight smile that said Natasha had done significant damage to my reputation with him, and I was going to have to work extra hard to fix it.

Once they were gone, Natasha straightened a little and fixed me with half-lidded eyes. "Well. That was great. Want me to take you to your place or the office?" Her words were slurred and she couldn't seem to fix her eyes on one spot for more than a few seconds. She was blasted.

It was a disaster. I'd foolishly thought I could keep her under control if I kept her by my side. Clearly, I'd underestimated her ability to disrupt my plans.

I could call someone to pick her up. William would do it, but I couldn't trust that asshole to keep dumb ideas from his head. He'd never take advantage of her while she was drunk like this, but I wouldn't put it past him to let her sleep on his couch and then make his move once she sobered up in the morning.

I'd been denying it, even to myself, but I knew this much. I didn't just want to keep my brother from Natasha. I wanted to keep everyone else from her. She was *my* problem. I wasn't going to call anyone from the office to take her home, because even when she was drunk out of her mind, she was the kind of woman men couldn't help falling in love with. Most men, at least. I only had to think about Valerie to remember exactly why I wasn't going anywhere near a relationship, let alone love.

I pulled her close to my side, leading her into the car when the valet pulled it up in front of the restaurant. I laid her in the back and set my jacket over her legs so she didn't end up flashing me through the rear-view, and I climbed in the driver seat. I had to call the office to get her address.

I cringed when I saw where she lived.

She lived in a mold-clad brick building that looked to be in the permanent shadow of the larger buildings around it. I'd have been shocked if an ounce of sunlight made it into her windows at any point in the day. It was a grim reminder of how far I'd come, and as much as Natasha was a thorn in my fucking side, I didn't like seeing her live here.

By the time I found a spot to park, I had to literally carry her two blocks to make it to the apartment. It was a statement on the type of neighborhood she lived in that nobody batted an eyelash to see me carrying her unconscious form with my jacket draped over her legs. She felt so small and fragile in my arms, and I couldn't help feeling a stab of longing at how good the contact felt. It had been two years since Valerie, but the pain still hung fresh enough to keep me firmly bound to the promise I made myself after it all ended.

No more relationships. No more commitments. No more trusting anyone I didn't have to.

I had to dig through Natasha's purse awkwardly with one hand while I tried to keep my grip on her with a raised knee and my free arm. I eventually found the keys to the front entrance and then found her apartment number that she had foolishly written on her keys in permanent marker. Didn't she realize some crazy asshole could find her keys and break into her apartment if she dropped these?

Of course, she didn't. If Natasha realized something like that, she wouldn't be the walking disaster-reel that she was.

A woman who couldn't have been over five foot and definitely wasn't a day under seventy years old burst out of the door across from Natasha's before I could go inside.

"Hmph," she said, jutting out her jaw and sizing me up. "She's got money to get drunk, but not to pay rent?"

"How much does she owe you?" I asked. Best to cut to the chase with people like this. I knew from experience.

I saw something in the woman's eyes that told me she smelled money, and she was quickly forming a plan to get as much as she possibly could. "Four months' rent. That's, um—" She frowned as she tried to do the mental math.

"Leave a note under her door within ten minutes that has your information. Make sure I can read it. I'll get you a check by tomorrow to cover what she owes."

The woman looked like she was about to claim Natasha owed even more money, but I let myself into Natasha's apartment before she had a chance. I'd be ripped off to some degree without a doubt, but it was harmless. One luxury of having excessive amounts of money is being able to value your time over almost any amount of money. If a few thousand dollars got me out of arguing with that woman for even a few minutes, it was a small price to pay.

It was a one bedroom with a cramped kitchen in the corner, a single window with a beautiful view of the dirty building just outside, and a bathroom that was hardly big enough for the door to swing open. Her bed was a few steps from the door. The place was an absolute mess, and a ridiculously chubby French Bulldog came charging at me as soon as I came inside. From the looks of it, the dog had also taken the liberty of having diarrhea all over. Judging by the smell, it was fresh.

I carefully set Natasha down on the bed, making sure I didn't step in any shit while I did. I knelt to let the dog sniff my hand. "I'm a good guy, don't worry. Your mommy might not agree, but it can be our little secret."

The dog cautiously sniffed my hand. After a few seconds, I passed the rigorous canine approval test and was rewarded with a wet lick to the chin.

"Was this you, or her?" I asked the dog as I surveyed the disgusting poop explosion. "Tell the truth."

The dog cowered a little, walking to go sit in the corner.

"Thought so," I said.

I rolled up my sleeves and spent the next half hour cleaning up shit. Thankfully, Natasha had hardwood floors, so it was nothing a little soap, water, and a hell of a lot of toilet paper couldn't handle. I tried propping her window open when I was done to let the place air out. It was hot outside this time of year, but a little heat would be better than the smell. I wasn't surprised to find her window was jammed closed.

With all the dog crap out of the way, I could see that her apartment was about as messy as I would've expected. She had a pile of laundry that wasn't folded but seemed to be clean sitting by the front door. I guessed it had probably absorbed the smell from her dog's accident and could use another wash.

I checked my watch. It was getting late, but I figured I could still hit a few stores before Natasha would wake. I'd grab her some toilet paper to replace the rolls I'd used cleaning up after her jumbo-sized bulldog, tools to fix her window, and I could stop by my place and wash her clothes.

I pulled off Natasha's shoes and put her blanket over her. I stopped for a few seconds to marvel at how innocent she looked when she was asleep. It was easy to forget this was the same woman who I didn't doubt had gotten drunk on purpose to teach me some kind of lesson. Leave it to her to use herself like a battering ram to get at me. She wasn't the subtle type, and I grudgingly had to admit I admired that about her. Maybe it was because her personality was about as far from Valerie's as you could get. Maybe it was just because she looked kind of adorable when she was trying her hardest to piss me off and only managing to endear herself to me.

I had expected something like this when I invited her to dinner, but I hadn't expected her to actually prove she was useful during the meeting. Someone was going to get their ass chewed out tomorrow for missing the WeConnect issue, but I was surprised Natasha knew the business world well enough to catch the problem. It could've been a fluke, but it was one I wasn't expecting. Even if we would've spotted it in a few weeks when we did the final review of the promotional plan, I was impressed.

I gently rolled her on her side and propped up some of her pillows behind her back and to make sure she wouldn't roll back over and risk throwing up while sleeping on her back.

"Keep an eye on her, okay?" I said to the dog. "And get out of the damn corner. You're not in trouble."

The dog happily got up and trotted over to jump on the bed and curl itself into a ball at Natasha's legs. He grunted at me.

"What?" I asked.

He grunted even harder, sitting up now and sticking his ridiculous underbite in my face. I took in the size of him and the folds of extra skin. "She spoils you, doesn't she. What are you expecting, a treat? Maybe that's why you have poop troubles, big guy. Tell you what, I'll get you a carrot from the store." I leaned down and scratched his blubbery face. "You want a carrot?"

He wagged his tail in confusion, but licked at my hands. I gave him a pat on the head. "Make sure she doesn't die. She's technically my employee and I don't feel like getting blamed for it. I'll come after you with my best lawyers if something happens to her."

7

NATASHA

I woke up with the kind of headache that makes you regret you ever existed. I didn't just want to die, I wanted to go back in time and stop my parents from ever making me in the first place.

My bout of melodrama subsided once I got a cup of coffee in my system and had a couple scrambled eggs. I was standing over the kitchen counter in a kind of mental haze the whole time I was cooking, meanwhile, Charlie wouldn't stop yapping at my ankles.

"No playing this morning, baby," I said to him. "I'm sorry. Mommy is hungover."

And then the memories came flooding back, bit by unpleasant bit. *Come on, big boy.* I had said that, hadn't I?

Then I had a near panic attack when I tried to figure out how I had gotten home. I remembered Bruce walking me out of the restaurant and *Oh God...* I remember the way I was clinging to him like some desperate drunk. I think I even squeezed his ass. My cheeks felt like they were on fire just at the memory.

I noticed Charlie actually hadn't pooped anywhere, which was a big relief. I never got a chance to come home and let him out, so I was going to give him a pass if he couldn't hold his little bladder anymore, and I definitely didn't walk him when I got home.

"I'm sorry, buddy," I said, kneeling to scratch his cheeks. "Let me just put this back and I'll get you outside. You must be about to burst." I noticed something out of the corner of my eye and turned to look at his doggy bed, where a full-sized carrot was sitting conspicuously. It looked real, too. Where the hell had he gotten a carrot?

I took the carton of eggs and opened the fridge. I set the eggs down next to the chicken and vegetables, and then did a double take. Chicken and vegetables?

I looked in the fridge for the first real time since waking up and saw it was stocked with enough food to last me through the week. The freezer was also full of meat and a few loaves of bread. I just stood there, staring in confusion at what had to be a couple hundred dollar's worth of groceries.

Then I noticed how neatly organized everything was, including the spare condiment containers I had probably kept around for several years now, because you never knew when you'd need some buffalo sauce. Every condiment container was organized in a color-coded system and from tallest to smallest. A quick glance around my apartment confirmed someone had gone through my stuff and organized everything. Including the stack of clean clothes I'd had on the floor that were now neatly folded in a pile outside my closet. My underwear was in that neatly folded pile, I noted.

Bruce.

It had to have been Bruce. He must have brought me home last night and then the state of my apartment had made some OCD wire in his brain catch on fire. But why had he bought me groceries? And from the amazing smell of the clothes he had folded, he had re-washed them with some kind of fancy detergent.

I almost got out the phone he had given me as his direct line and called him, but before I could dial his number, I saw what time it was.

I was already an hour late and I hadn't even left the house.

I scooped up Charlie, sprinted down the stairs, set him down and let him do his business on the small patch of grass out front, and then ran him back upstairs like he was a football and I was a star running-back. I was shocked when my landlord didn't take the opportunity to bust out of her room and harass me about rent, but I wasn't about to complain.

I took the world's fastest shower, threw on clothes and under-wear while I tried not to blush at the thought that Bruce now had about a one in ten chance of guessing what color my panties were on any given day. I gave Charlie a quick kiss, and I sprinted outside. Bruce had found a really good parking spot right in front, which was thankful, because I was worried I'd have to hunt around the block for the car.

I only thought to check the phone Bruce had given me once I was in the car. I had a text from him.

Bruce: Don't need picked up today. Meet at the office. Bring the banana.

Relief and a little bit of confusion ran through me. He had clearly been the one to make sure I got safely back to my bed last night, and he *definitely* was the one who was such a compulsive organizer that he had hit my apartment like a reverse tornado. I was reluctant to call any of it kindness, because I wasn't sure Mr. Sex Robot was capable of kindness. He had to have rationalized it in some weird, coldly logical way as a thing he had to do. Maybe he just figured he couldn't torture his intern if she drunkenly wandered into the street and got hit by a car, or if she died of malnutrition via ramen noodle overdose. The organization had probably been a compulsion and not an attempt at being helpful. He probably organized store shelves when he went shopping, too.

I opened the door to Bruce's office just past ten in the morning. It was late, even by my standards. I stuck out the banana I'd picked up on the way like it was a peace offering.

Bruce stood, grabbed it, and promptly dropped it into the trash without giving it more than a quick skim with his eyes.

I blew out a breath. It wasn't exactly a sigh, but it was close. "What was wrong with that one?"

"It was late."

"Then why did you ask me to bring one?"

"I don't need a good reason, *intern*," He let the word pass those luscious lips of his with a slow, deliberate bite to it.

"Right." I tried to keep my face a perfect blank, not wanting him to feel the satisfaction of getting to me. "Remind me, do you want your coffee with or without spit this morning?"

"Chef's choice."

I made an annoyed noise and stormed out of his office to make his cup of coffee. He had a talent for reminding me to hate him just when I started to get confused. It would serve him right if I really did spit in it, but he seemed to be calling my bluff. There was a level of wrong I wasn't willing to cross, even to piss him off when he deserved it so badly. I settled for something less disgusting and dumped a packet of sugar in his coffee. I even added a splash of milk, hoping the bastard was lactose intolerant and had to disrupt his perfect schedule with a trip to the bathroom.

Okay, arguably, it was probably worse than spitting in his coffee. But all I had to do was remember the subtle look of gloating victory in his eyes when he threw away the banana.

I STEPPED BACK IN HIS OFFICE, CATCHING HIM ON A PHONE CALL. I handed him the coffee and stood just in front of him as he bent his neck to take a sip.

There was a sound like a pipe springing a leak and I was suddenly bathed in a mist of warm liquid.

I looked down, not understanding how little dots of brown had suddenly appeared on my blouse and face. Then I saw the look of horror in Bruce's eyes.

"Shit," he said. He grabbed a handful of napkins from a drawer in his desk and started dabbing at my face and then my blouse.

We both froze when we seemed to realize at the same time that he was pressing a tissue to my breast. I looked up at Bruce, who was looking at his own hand almost in confusion, but desire was clear in his features.

"If you wanted to grope me," I said through a tight, nervous throat. "You didn't have to spit coffee on me."

He pulled his hand back, and for the first time since I'd met him, he actually smiled. It was a good smile. It was the kind of smile that made your heart melt and made girls fall in love. It was self-deprecating, genuine, and so, so sexy. And the way his eyes flicked up to meet mine, twinkling with what I could've almost called mischief was the cherry on top. "Sugar," he said.

"Yes?" I asked.

He frowned at me, then put a hand up to cover his widening smile and laughed.

"Oh," I blurted, "Oh, yes. Yes. I put sugar in the coffee." I had thought he was calling *me* sugar, and I actually answered to it? *My God.*

He still wore that gorgeous smile as he looked down at me and set his coffee on the table. "So," he said. "Is that what you'd like me to call you instead of intern? *Sugar?*"

A blush exploded through me. I hung my head, torn between laughing and crying. "Actually, I'd just like to know where the best place to curl up and die of embarrassment is. Know anywhere nice?"

"You could come under my desk," he said.

I wasn't sure if he meant it as flirtation or not, but from the way he tensed after a few seconds, I thought it was unintentional.

"I don't think that would be a good idea right now. I'd get into trouble down there."

He raised an eyebrow. "What kind of trouble could you possibly get into under my desk?"

"They say once an intern gets a taste of their boss' banana, they never really stop craving it." I tried to stop myself from saying it, I really did, but he had set me up far, far too perfectly for the dirty joke. I owed it to the universe to say it.

I expected him to laugh or even to act disappointed, but I only saw that same heat and intensity spark up in his eyes from when he was pressing the napkin to my breast.

He took half a step toward me, and for a crazy moment, I thought he was going to pin me to the door and kiss me. For an equally crazy second, I thought I wanted him to.

I cleared my throat and reached past him to pick up the coffee. "I'll fix this. I'm sorry," I said quickly and turned to half-run back to the break room.

I leaned against the wall in the break room a minute later and blew out a long, calming breath while a new pot of coffee brewed. I jumped when I thought I saw Bruce come strolling in, but something was off about him. Then it clicked. The messy hair. No tie. A few buttons undone. It was William.

"It's the prodigal intern," he said cheerily. "Tell me. Does my brother let you make coffee for other people, or does he want you all to himself?"

"He doesn't own me," I said a little more bitterly than I intended to. "I mean. I can make you a cup, if you like."

William nodded, but the grin he wore was far too knowing for my liking. "What happened to you. Tried to take a coffee shower? With your clothes on?"

"Your brother apparently doesn't like the taste of sugar."

William squinted his eyes, as if he didn't fully understand but didn't completely care. "So," he said, crossing his arms and leaning in the doorway. "What's your story, anyway? Why is Bruce so interested in you?"

"Did he say something?" I asked, hating how hopeful I sounded.

William's grin widened. "You know what, nevermind. I can see the whole picture here." He laughed softly. "By the way, did you realize you've only been wearing pencil skirts since I told you my brother has a fetish for them? Naughty little intern, you."

I blushed deeply. I couldn't lie and say it was a coincidence. "I have a limited wardrobe."

"Right. Well, since you're definitely not secretly hoping to seduce my brother, I guess you wouldn't be interested in his one glaring weakness."

I tried so hard not to ask, but I couldn't do it. "What is it?"

"A banana split. The guy would sell his soul for bananas and ice cream."

I made a skeptical face. "I can't picture him eating ice cream."

"Well, believe it or not, he wasn't always so uptight. A girl royally fucked him over, and his whole 'never make the same mistake twice' thing kind of went on the fritz. He has been pretty unbearable ever since. I've been waiting for him to get tired of it, but he hasn't shown any signs of slowing down."

"I see. And you're supplying me with his kryptonite because you're hoping I'll sleep with him and loosen him up? That's sick. You realize that, right?"

"Hey, there's nothing sick about two consenting adults having sex. And there's nothing sick about a man's brother wanting to do what's best for him. Just think it over. He needs it. You'd be doing a public service for both of us."

I made a disgusted sound. "Even if I *had* secretly thought about sleeping with him, which I haven't, you just made it so weird I could never do it."

William dismissed my concerns with a flap of his hand and that grin he wore so easily. "It's uncomfortable when someone sees right through all your pretenses. I get it. I'll take my coffee and get out of your hair. But just remember. Banana split. Oh, and he likes dirty talk. Remember that. Drives him wild."

William actually winked at me after I poured his coffee.

I stared at the coffee pot for a few minutes before I mustered up the strength to go back into Bruce's office. I didn't appreciate William and his cocky surety that I really was interested in Bruce. I had never fully come out of the high school mindset that sex was something special. Most of the women I knew, especially being in New York, took a much more liberal approach to sex. For them, it was a fun pastime. Something to do for a night as long as the guy clearly wasn't a creeper and was clean.

I wasn't even sure what had triggered me to make it into something so sacred and mystical. Yeah, I'd slept with a couple guys before. Okay, *one* guy. But I'd seen plenty of movies and heard the war stories from friends. I had a first-hand experience with exactly how fast a man can reach orgasm and the deep, dirty shame I felt afterwards when it was over.

I met the guy who took my virginity on a dating site after my college friends had bullied me into making a profile. We went out three times, and all my friends were telling me date number three basically has an unwritten requirement to end in sex if things are going well. I had felt weird about it. *So* weird. The guy was cute and we got along okay, but it hadn't felt like the right time. Still, I went through with it. All thirty seconds of it.

I broke things off shortly after because the sex felt like it high-lighted all the future problems I'd have with him. It was probably an overreaction, but it was the way I felt, and intimacy had intimi-dated me ever since.

And then there was Bruce.

If William thought I was seriously considering trying to sleep with the man, he really wasn't even close to understanding me. I had enough trouble imagining sex with a guy I'd been dating—a guy I was getting along with. But Bruce?

Sex with him would be... hateful? I wasn't sure. The only ways I can imagine it happening were rough and raw and intense. It wouldn't be anything like the candlelit romantic pleasure cruise I had gradually built up as my ideal sexual fantasy. And yet I couldn't help feeling a cold shiver that quickly turned into warmth every time I thought about how his arms would be like steel, how strangely good it would feel to have some kind of power over a man who seemed to have the world at his feet. I kept thinking about how strangely wonderful it would feel to grip his length and watch all the power drain out of him, transferred to me as I took the captain's seat in his life, even if it was just for a while.

I groaned out loud. Maybe William wasn't completely wrong, but he was still crude and he was still an ass.

I shook the thoughts from my head. I had a job to do.

I knew Bruce would be getting impatient already for his coffee. I wouldn't put it past him to know exactly how long the walk to the break room takes and how long it takes to brew a fresh cup of coffee. He'd probably be able to tell me exactly how many seconds longer I had taken than I should've. He could deal with it though, and if he really cared to ask, I'd tell him I was in the bathroom.

I loitered in the break room for another minute or so until a pair of women came in.

"Don't even ask about the Murdoch account," said the older of the two women. She wore a rueful smile. "You'll just remind him and we'll all end up stuck here for the weekend until we get it sorted out."

"Ugh," said the other, who was helping herself to coffee. "You're probably right."

The woman with the coffee noticed me then. She was a few inches taller than me and looked to be in her thirties with a pretty, freckle-smeared nose and brown hair. "You're Bruce's new intern, right?" she asked.

"Yep," I said. "Word has already spread, I guess?"

She nodded. "Bruce has never made a secret of how much he hates the idea of interns, and I've never known him to have one, so yeah. People were naturally pretty curious when you showed up."

She paused, and I realized she was waiting for me to explain what the real story was. I also realized she and most of the office must have their own explanation already. They thought I was sleeping with him, or that he was hoping to sleep with me. I wished I could brush off the way their assumption stung, but I couldn't. All these people I'd never even met were so ready to assume I fell neatly into the stereotype of the young intern looking to get ahead. I guessed I shouldn't be too surprised. It was easier to think the worst of someone you didn't know than to bother learning the truth.

I made an effort at a polite smile and laughed a little. It seemed like the best way to diffuse the situation without having to explain the truth, which was probably too ridiculous to believe anyway. *He caught me eating his banana and he hired me to punish me.*

"So?" she asked. She wasn't going to let me off easy, apparently. "Are you two... *you know.*"

"No, no. Definitely not." I tried to scrunch my face up to show just how crazy that idea was. "Absolutely not."

"Are you in a relationship, then?"

"Nope," I said, even though I was quickly reaching the point of wanting to tell this nosy woman to shove her fifty questions up her butt and leave me alone.

The other woman who had come in with her had picked up on the conversation, and leaned in a little bit. "If Bruce Chamberson wanted me to be his intern just for sex, I wouldn't fight it."

The woman with the coffee laughed in surprise. "Stacy! You're married."

Stacy shrugged. "If Michael saw Bruce, he'd understand. Though to be honest, I think I'd have more fun with William."

The woman nodded. "Sure. But if you wanted an actual relationship, I think Bruce would be the better bet. William would be the one if you wanted something with no strings attached. Bruce strikes me as the type who would get really possessive." She thought about that, then crinkled her eyes and grinned. "In the sexy man-bear kind of way."

Stacy laughed, and I started to feel like my chance to slip out of the conversation was here.

"Well, I've got to get back to the *man-bear*," I said.

Both women laughed.

"Oh to be young again," said Stacy as I was leaving the break room, even though she couldn't have been more than a few years my senior.

I did my best to gather my wits on the way back to Bruce's office. It was only my first week, and I already felt like I'd been sucked into something far more turbulent and out of my control than I expected. I could quickly feel my own emotions getting tangled into this, into what was supposed to be a job. Candace seemed to think I was crazy for not wanting to sleep with Bruce. The women in the break room clearly did. Even Bruce's brother was pretty much telling me to sleep with him.

I was starting to think Bruce and I were the only people on the Earth who *didn't* want us to sleep together. But if I was honest with myself, I wasn't sure that was true. The look in Bruce's eyes floated into my thoughts, and I couldn't forget the way his touch on my breast had ignited something in me that still felt like it was raging deep down.

Getting dirt on Bruce might be the least of my challenges. It was starting to seem like I was also going to have to figure out how the hell I'd deal with my growing, confusing feelings toward him.

8

BRUCE

I t was such a picturesque day that it could make me sick. Birds were chirping, the grass on the golf course was green and perfectly manicured. A man-made outcropping of rocks lined the lake, which was home to a flock of ducks that occasionally dunked their heads underwater to snag a juicy bit of whatever it was ducks ate. Even the weather was nice.

I stepped out of the golf cart and looked at my caddy, who was actually wearing the hat I'd told her to wear, much to my surprise. "Five-iron, please."

Natasha looked like she would rather bash me over the head with a golf club than hand me one. "And which one is that, master?" she asked sarcastically.

"The one with a five on it. No wonder I don't pay you."

She slid the club out of the bag and walked toward me with a look of pure fire in her eyes. I tried not to notice the way her hips swayed in the boyish khaki pants she wore, or the way her black polo fit her form so well and gave me a tantalizing glimpse of her cleavage. She looked absolutely ridiculous in the floppy hat I'd told her she had to wear to be my caddy, but it was admittedly a cute kind of ridiculous. The hat was the kind every guy wore back in the fifties.

I took the club from her, feeling a flicker of excitement when our fingers touched.

It was strange, with her, my desire to purge her from my life only got stronger the longer I spent with her. She'd been working for me over a week now, and I'd already lost count of how many times she had fucked up my routine. Yet at the same time, a strange, confusing part of me kind of enjoyed the challenge of bringing her in line. There might have even been a protective part of me that felt a need to save her from herself. After all, I'd seen how likely she was to fall down a flight of stairs or walk into traffic by mistake. Keeping her at my side might have been more about keeping her alive than it was about whatever this strange game we were playing was.

"Remind me again how this counts as a business event?" she asked.

"Well," I said. "See those men over there?" I pointed to Alec and Von, who were playing the hole behind us a few hundred yards away. "Those are two Swedish entrepreneurs who are looking to launch a chain of restaurants in the U.S. Word is, their goal is to be nationwide within five years. I want them to choose Galleon, so I show up to the same golf outing as them. I give them their space, but let them see me around—by coincidence, of course. When everyone stops to grab a few drinks in the club-house after our round, who knows, maybe we'll end up talking some business with them."

"And you needed to dress me up like a clown to accomplish that?" I asked.

"To be honest? I didn't think you'd actually wear the clothes I had Linda bring you."

I'd seen Natasha blush plenty of times, but the red that flushed her face now might have been the first angry blush I'd seen.

I couldn't help grinning a little, which felt strange. I'd never been the type to smile easily or find amusement in much of anything. At least not since Valerie.

"You know," she said, words laced with anger. "Everybody in your office thinks you're just keeping me around as a kind of sex slave. Dressing me up like this isn't going to help dispel the rumors."

"So what if they do? It'll keep any of the guys in the office from thinking it'd be a good idea to hit on you."

"What?" she asked. "No one is allowed to hit on me, now?"

"Unless they want to be fired, no. They had better not."

She folded her arms over her chest, which had the incidental effect of pressing her breasts together in a distracting way. "Is that part of my punishment, then? You want to make sure I can't even hope to meet a guy while I'm your slave?"

"No. It's because you work for me. You're mine. I don't want anybody touching what's mine. Simple as that."

"Yours?" she asks incredulously. "And what happens if I don't want to be a dusty trophy on your shelf?"

"Then you can quit. Until then, you are playing by my rules."

"You're a real bastard. You know that?" She pressed her lips together in an angry line, looked at my golf bag, and then hopped in the golf cart and sped off. I watched after her, nearly laughing out loud when she had to drive a loop and come back after a few seconds. She got out of the cart angrily, rifled through the pouch on the front of my golf bag, and snatched the keys out. "I forgot these. Okay?" she snapped, face blazing red, and then she got back in the cart and drove off.

I shook my head. The damn woman really had a way of pissing me off and intriguing me at the same time.

IT WAS ALMOST NINE IN THE EVENING AND I WAS STILL AT THE office. I did everything I could to keep my life to a strict schedule, but staying late for work was a surprisingly small disruption to my routine, and it was one I didn't mind.

The difference was that Natasha was still in the office, too, meaning the entire building was empty except for cleaning staff, myself, and the intern.

I was at my desk, trying to make sure I had the last details perfectly in place for a briefing with one of our biggest clients tomorrow. My stomach was rumbling because I'd actually lost track of the dinner I'd packed. I was sure I left it in the break room fridge, but when I checked for it at my usual dinner time thirty minutes ago, it was gone.

Natasha stuck her head in the office. "You realize I'm not working out here, right? You've never actually given me any kind of job except to follow you around and annoy you, so I was wondering if I could go home yet."

I glared at her. She'd already asked about three times to go home for the evening, and I was almost ready to give in and let her go. I was starting to doubt my own motives for keeping her around and punishing her. The incident with the banana was days ago now, and if I was being completely honest, I knew I'd probably put her through more than enough to make up for it by now. But it wasn't that simple anymore.

I took in her chestnut hair and brown eyes as she dangled in the doorway, sticking only her head and shoulders in my office like she thought she might need to make a quick escape if things turned south.

"There's actually one thing you could do before you go," I said. "Go get some Chinese for us or something."

She stepped in the room then, widening her eyes and covering her mouth in an exaggerated portrayal of shock. "*You?* Eating takeout food? Aren't you worried you're going to turn into a ball of blubber and I'll have to roll you out of the office tonight?"

"I eat the way I do because I want my mind sharp. The right

nutrients at the right time of day keep your energy levels stable and your mood good."

She raised an eyebrow. "So that's the problem then. Your nutrients must be way off, because I don't think I've ever seen you in a good mood, except when you were groping me that one time."

I couldn't remember the last time I'd blushed, but I thought I felt a little bit of warmth spreading in my cheeks then. "I wasn't *groping* you. I was trying to get the coffee out of your shirt before it stained."

"Right. You just started with my boobs."

"They were the... closest thing I could reach."

She blew out a surprised laugh and fixed me with an intoxicating smile. "Is what your brother says true? About your secretary fetish?"

"I've never had a secretary fetish."

"Past tense," she noted.

I grinned. "Listen. If you want to interview me, you'd better go get some food. Quickly. I think we have about ten minutes before the only noises I can make are frothing and growling sounds. I don't handle hungry well."

"I'm pretty sure frothing doesn't make a sound, for the record."

She saw the look on my face and raised her hands defensively. "Okay, okay. What do you want from the Chinese place?"

"Anything, but make sure you get crab rangoons. I haven't had them in years and I think I'd do anything for one right now."

"Anything?" she asked with a mischievous little sparkle in her eye.

SHE CAME BACK THIRTY MINUTES LATER WITH TWO HUGE BROWN BAGS full of food. It was the worst kind of food in a nutritional sense. I thought my dietician would probably have a heart attack if she saw, and I was sure I'd feel like shit the next morning, but for some reason I didn't care. Maybe it was just the ravenous hunger in my stomach, or maybe Natasha, the walking disaster, was rubbing off on me.

I started pulling out containers while I looked for the crab rangoons and then realized Natasha was just watching me.

"What?" I asked.

"I feel like I need to call your handler or something. Are you sure nothing is wrong?"

I set down the waxy paper bag filled with rangoons and shrugged. "Why would something be wrong?"

"Oh," she said casually. "No idea."

I bit into the rangoon and leaned back in my chair, smiling as I chewed. "Damn, these are good. I used to get them all the time in college. Some places make them into kind of a wing shape with a pocket of filling at the bottom and a big crusty flap at the top. But these? These are the best kind." I turned over the rangoon in my fingers, showing her the four, smaller pointed tips of crunchy pastry that spiked up from the juicy and crunchy pocket of crab and cream-filled deliciousness at the center.

"I'm glad you like them."

"Are you going to eat, or are you just going to stand there being weird?"

She sighed, sat down, and opened the most boring container she possibly could. It was just a bunch of plain white rice. It seemed like something was bothering her, but I wasn't sure if I was exactly the person she would prefer to confide in, so I settled for enjoying the meal across from her for a few minutes without making any conversation.

She eventually looked up from the rice, which she was barely touching. Her forehead was knotted together. "What was the deal with everything you did at my apartment?" she asked.

The question surprised me. I set down the stick of skewered beef I'd been working on. "It was nothing."

"No. Nothing would've been using your bazillions of dollars to call some personal assistant to come dump me back at my place. What you did was actually considerate. And you gave my dog a carrot. I know you did, so don't even try to deny it."

"Was the carrot the tipping point, or?"

"No," she said. "There's no *tipping point*. I'm just tired of thinking I have a read on you and then you go and do something that doesn't make any sense. You hire me to punish me. You practically force me to be your slave. You demean me whenever you get a chance. Then you also make dirty jokes, flirt with me, *grope me*, and do something confusingly considerate when I get blackout drunk. You even fixed my stupid window in the kitchen that never opened." She gave a defeated kind of shrug. "I'm just tired of it. I want to know if I'm supposed to hate you or like you, and you're making me feel like the emotional equivalent of a pinball."

I leaned back in my chair. "A pinball between hate and like," I said. "So that means you like me, at times?"

She rolled her eyes in that way she had. It wasn't disrespectful or immature like it would be from someone else. It was playful and sexy. It made it feel like we were in on some joke together. "It also means I hate you, at times."

Warning bells were going off in my brain. *Disengage. Abort. End this. Now.*

The security system I'd spent two years building inside my body wanted to do anything to keep me from taking this conversation any farther, but Natasha had a way of bypassing all of that. I couldn't control myself around her. Not always.

"Well," I said. "That makes two of us."

She flashed a half-smile. "So that means you like me, at times?"

"At times," I said. "And generally at the times when it doesn't make any goddamn sense."

She chewed her lip. "When was a time that you liked me, for curiosity's sake, of course."

"When you had the balls to point out the schedule conflict with WeConnect at dinner. When you wore the ridiculous caddy outfit I asked you to wear. When you tried to slip sugar into my coffee. *When I could tell you were turned on when I was cleaning that coffee off your... shirt.*"

She lowered her eyes and took in a deep, shuddering kind of breath. "And how could you tell I was turned on?"

"The same way I can tell now," I said. "You're hardly breathing or blinking. Your cheeks and chest are red. You're sitting as straight as an arrow. Every part of your body is on high-alert. I bet your skin feels like it's prickling with electricity."

She absently rubbed her hand over her arm, where the hairs were standing on end and her skin was rising with goosebumps. "Wrong," she said quietly. "It's more like sunlight. Like there's a warm light making me feel hot all over." She paused, looking up at me and chewing her lip again in a way that had me seriously questioning all the promises I'd made myself about avoiding complications.

"And this warm feeling," I said. "What does it make you want to do?"

She grinned. "Honestly? It's making me crave bananas."

I felt jarred out of the moment by the sheer ridiculousness of it. "What?" I asked.

"Something cold. Like the banana split I picked up after I got the Chinese. I left it in the break room and there's enough for two."

9

NATASHA

I saw Bruce Chamberson smile for the second time since I'd met him when I pulled the banana split out of the freezer. Thankfully, it'd only been in there about twenty minutes, and the bananas were still the perfect temperature. It was a monster of a split. There were two bananas on either side of three mounds of chocolate, strawberry, and vanilla ice cream. The entire beast was covered generously in whipped cream, chocolate syrup over the chocolate ice cream, strawberry syrup over the strawberry ice cream, and a caramel drizzle over the vanilla.

"You've been talking to William, haven't you," said Bruce.

"Maybe," I admitted.

Bruce gave me a look that could've had a nun stripping out of her robe in an instant. It was pure sex. Pure fire. "The last time William talked someone into getting me a banana split, he told me he had said it'd get them in my pants. Does this mean you're hoping to get into my pants?"

"That would be crazy," I said quickly. "I'd never fit."

He burst out laughing. He had a good laugh. It was an honest laugh. Infectious, even. I smiled along, watching him to wait for his next move. Whatever was happening, the ball was in his court. I may have dragged us to the court to begin with, but I knew it was up to him from here, and I was glad for it. I still wasn't sure where I really wanted this all to go. The only thing I knew was there was no use fighting my attraction to him. Who knew if a relationship would ever work between us, but it was like Candace said. I was a big girl. I didn't have to like him to sleep with him.

But it would've been easier if I knew I didn't like him. The problem was that I wasn't so sure anymore. I found myself thinking of him all the time. I craved those glimpses of happiness he'd sometimes let slip. I liked being the cause of that, feeling like I had some kind of special effect on him.

He didn't waste any time digging into the desert, but he did make sure I got a spoon as well and could share. It felt intimate, sharing the desert with him, especially when he kept making the most adorable and somehow sexy noises of enjoyment. It was like he couldn't help himself.

"You have any family?" he asked. The question came out of nowhere, but when I realized we'd just been stuffing our faces for close to five minutes, I guessed he might have started wondering about me. All he knew was what he saw. Bruce knew next to nothing about my home life, my past, or my family. It was a little flattering that he was curious.

"Yep," I said, licking the back of my spoon clean and sighing. I set it down, because I didn't want to feel bloated and gross in front of Bruce, no matter how much I wanted to keep eating. "My mom and dad live outside the city. They're teachers. My older brother lives with them."

Bruce gave the nod I was used to seeing when I revealed that little tidbit about my brother. It was a kind of mixture between sympathy and curiosity.

"He never really found his direction in life," I explained. "He spends all his energy on get rich quick schemes. He's tried the multi-level marketing stuff. Once he was running a kind of scam where he'd list items for sale that he found on big store's websites at a markup. Like if they were selling mittens for two dollars, he'd list a bunch of them on eBay for four, and then once someone placed the order, he'd go drive up, buy the stuff, package it, and sell it for a profit. I'm pretty sure it was illegal, but his account got shut down for some other stupid thing he did, anyway."

"I've known the type," said Bruce. "My parents are a little bit like that. They think William and I are their personal, bottomless ATM machines. Forget the fact that they did just about everything in their power to stop us from getting where we are in the first place. Now that we're here, it's thanks to them, of course."

"That can't be easy. I've thought about it before," I said. "How it'd be hard to make it big at something. Pretty soon, you'd realize almost everyone you knew was just after their own piece of what you had."

He laughed, but it was a sad sound, and the way his eyes went distant told me I'd struck a chord. "Is that what happened?" I asked. "With the girl, I mean. The one your brother mentioned."

Bruce seemed to think about my question for a long time. I wasn't sure if he was deciding whether to answer or trying to find the right way. "It's not really something I want to think about right now," he said finally.

I nodded quickly, and in my hurry to apologize for asking such a nosy question, my hand catapulted his spoon out of the dessert dish, spraying both of us with bits of ice cream and syrup from the base of the bowl. I looked down at his lap in horror at the three large spots of ice cream, one of each flavor, quickly seeping into his expensive pants.

I half-reached to wipe it away before I realized I'd be the one doing the groping if I did.

He looked down at my hand, watching as I pulled it back awkwardly and blushed like an idiot.

With no apparent hurry, he swiped up a bead of the melting chocolate ice cream on his index finger, inspected it, and then extended his finger toward my mouth. "Are you going to clean up your mess, intern?" His voice was a deep, sexy rasp, and there was no mistaking the way his eyelids looked almost heavy beneath those thick eyelashes.

Did he want me to... *Oh, God.* I felt immediately and totally sexually inadequate. I wanted this. I knew I did. It wasn't awkward college-level sexual tension. This was real. The big leagues, and I had never been aware of how woefully unprepared I was for this.

"Uh," I stammered, reaching for a napkin.

"No," he said firmly. "Not with the napkin."

I swallowed hard and lifted my fingertips to his wrist, where I pulled him closer to my mouth, inch by nervous inch. I brought the tip of his finger into my mouth, letting my lips wrap around it. All my uncertainty and nerves were blasted away when I saw the look on his face. He was rapt with pleasure, absolutely over the edge with need and desire.

It felt like I could bring him to his knees with the slightest movement of my tongue, and I thought I could get drunk on power like that.

I pulled away from his finger, my hand still on his wrist, and when our eyes met it sent a jolt of pure fire lancing through me. "I don't... This isn't the kind of thing I do," I said.

"So you just make messes and don't clean them up?" he asked.

I looked down at his finger, smirking a little. "I don't typically use my mouth, especially when the mess is on someone else's crotch."

"Typically? So you do at times, just not always?"

"Believe it or not, this is a first."

"Good," he said. "I like the idea of having you to myself."

His words sent a warm tingle across my skin, like they were a spell that bound me to him in some way. I wasn't sure how he intended them. I knew our bodies were both probably moving on auto-pilot at this point, drawing us closer and closer to the inevitable, but I didn't know what happened after that. If I believed Candace, I wasn't supposed to care. It was just supposed to be sex. Just fun.

That wasn't enough for me, though.

"Is this a good idea?" I asked.

He was standing now. His body was so close to mine I could feel the heat radiating off of him. I wondered if I'd feel the hardness of his arousal if he moved another inch closer.

Bruce brought his fingers to my cheek, letting them drift from my jaw to my chin as he traced a path and followed it intently with his eyes, almost like he expected to find something there. "Maybe not," he said. "Maybe you're just after my money, and maybe I'm just looking for a taste of you before I'll toss you aside. But we could talk about it for days and we still wouldn't know unless we tried."

I leaned forward, letting my forehead touch his chest as my thoughts raced. "How do I know you're not after *my* money?" I asked after a while.

His chuckle rumbled through his chest. "I guess you're going to have to ask yourself a very important question. Do you feel lucky, intern? Huh, do ya?"

I looked up at him with a half-smile. "Right now? Yes. For once, I do."

He kissed me then, and it was more than I thought it could've been. The world closed in around us. The distant sound of cars rumbling across the street and wind against the windows and the air conditioner all blurred until they were nothing. It was like every sensory nerve in my body except my lips and hands shut off to focus as much as possible on the places where he and I met.

His lips were so unbelievably warm and soft, with just enough wet to keep from feeling dry but not so much to seem sloppy. I could taste the faint sweet tang of our desert on his lips and tongue. He kissed me like he'd been waiting since the first moment he saw me. He advanced on me, holding me by the shoulders to keep from knocking me over as he backed me up to the break room door and pinned me there.

I felt his hand thump against the door beside my head. His other hand threaded through my hair until he had a grip of my hair and he could tilt my face up more to meet his. The solid warmth of his body was flush against mine, and I could feel the distinct pressure of his arousal digging into my stomach.

"My brother was right," he breathed between kisses. "But not exactly."

"About what?" I asked. My hands were moving on their own, shamelessly exploring every bulge, curve, and crease of his sculpted body that I could feel through his dress shirt. I ached to strip it off him, but I was in uncharted waters. I wanted to let him take the lead. I wanted to trust him to guide me through this.

"About the pencil skirts and the secretary look. But it's not a fetish. I just couldn't stop thinking about hiking those skirts up and spreading you out, making you moan my name until your voice was hoarse."

I gulped, forgetting to kiss him back for a few seconds as the dirty sting of his words worked its magic on me, from my tingling fingertips to the way warmth was exploding in my lower belly. And then, with the suddenness of a cold hand gripping my ankle from the darkness, reality broke through the moment. I needed to admit the truth to him. I couldn't do *this* while still planning to write my story. He had to know.

"Bruce, there's something—"

"If this is the part where you admit you're a Russian spy sent to kill me," he said, cutting me off. "Save it. I don't care. Not right now."

I tried to will myself to say it anyway. I really tried, but every time he kissed me or felt hungrily at me with those big hands of his, I was torn back into his dream world, the strange place where it didn't seem to matter that I had bills to pay and the only way they were getting paid was if I could betray Bruce. All that mattered here was what felt good and what was natural. And *God,* I'd never understood the meaning of natural until his hands were on me and my mouth was against his. There was nothing more natural in the world than taking more, *craving* more.

He picked me up, still stealing kisses even as he hauled me with my legs wrapped around his waist to the table overlooking the indoor gardens in the courtyard below. My skirt was bunched up around my waist and, to my horror, I realized I was wearing what had to be the least sexy pair of panties I owned. They were a kind of unflattering grass green with pulled threads in the fabric. Worst of all, they were a little big on me and had the definite granny panty factor going for them.

To my relief, Bruce, Mr. Control and Mr. Calm, decided to go full barbarian. Without taking his lips from mine, he reached down, took the waistband of my panties in his fist, and pulled. They didn't snap off, they *ripped* off.

I gasped into his mouth and gripped the back of his neck, digging my fingernails into his skin.

"Hope you didn't like those," he grunted, and I thought I almost sensed surprise in his voice, like he wasn't expecting to feel so out of control. It comforted me a little to think I wasn't the only one who felt pulled along by some invisible but overpowering current.

"They were my favorites," I lied. "I'm going to sue you now."

"I understand now," he said, gently forcing me to lay my back down on the table with my legs spread around him. "You *were* after my money this whole time. This was all an elaborate setup to get me to tear off your panties and land me in court."

I licked my lips, too turned on to fully dive into the act of teasing him. "That's right," I said breathily. "Putting your banana in my mouth was just the first step in a long, complicated dance you didn't know you were part of. I'm actually a mastermind, not a clutz."

He chuckled, but the arousal in his system wiped the amusement from his face in an instant, as if he could only momentarily distract himself from what was in front of him. *From me.* "You almost had me going until you tried to claim you weren't a clutz."

"Damn," I said. "My cover is blown, I guess."

He stole the breath straight out of my lungs when he reached for his tie and stripped it free in one smooth motion. His eyes never left mine, and *God* did they hold all the dirty promises eyes could possibly hold. He knew his slow, unhurried pace was torture for me as I laid there helplessly exposed before him, but he showed no mercy.

He undid each button with deliberate movements that seemed to take forever.

One button. The top of his tanned chest and a hint of his clavicle.

Two buttons. A deep crease running between his pecs and a hint of the raised muscle of his chest.

Three buttons. The distinct line where his pecs end and the first pair of perfectly defined abs.

He never made it to four, because I lost my patience. I sat myself up, grabbed both sides of his shirt, and spread it wide. I didn't care if I popped buttons in the process. He had destroyed my panties, after all. Forget the fact that his shirt probably cost a hundred dollars and my panties were a bargain bin steal—that wasn't the point.

He made a sound somewhere between a growl and a grunt as the shirt tore free and I got a front-row seat to the kind of body you normally only saw on big screens or in fashion magazines. "Well, there goes your legal grounds, intern," he said.

"Fuck the money. I just want you."

I didn't have to wonder if my words had any effect on him, because he stripped out of his pants and tore off the rest of my clothes in what felt like milliseconds. In an instant, we were both completely bare. I might've felt self-conscious, but the way his eyes were drinking me in left no room for doubt. He liked what he saw.

I knew some girls looked at porn, but I'd always felt weird about it. Consequently, I'd only seen one guy naked before, and it was safe to say, I hadn't fully understood that the guy I had been with must've been on the very small side. That, or Bruce was fortunate. Very fortunate.

I expected him to try to slide himself in right away, but instead he knelt down in front of the table. I half-sat and had to fight the urge to press my legs together. It was one thing to be naked in front of him, it was another to have his face just inches from my most intimate places. He didn't give me time to worry about it though, because when his lips met my inner thigh, all my worries melted away in a rush of white-hot pleasure.

I leaned back on my elbows, not wanting to lay completely flat because the sight of him doing his work was too hot to close my eyes or look away.

"You don't have to..." I was barely speaking above a whisper, and I didn't know why I was trying to talk him out of it when every cell in my body was screaming for him to keep going.

He met my eyes as he slowly ran the flat of his tongue from my inner thigh to my pussy. My mouth shot open in a silent gasp and my body tensed. I was left gasping from just a few seconds of the intimate contact, and absolutely famished for more.

"You want me to stop, then?" he asked with a cocky grin.

"Don't you dare."

He buried his face between my legs and went to work on me like I was the most delicious thing he'd ever tasted. I gripped his hair, the table, his shoulders, and whatever else I could get a hold of.

He used his lips, the tip of his tongue, the base of his tongue, and his fingers. They all worked together in a kind of choreography that felt designed to melt me from the inside out. A kind of pressure like I'd never felt before was building inside me, and it felt so strong I was almost afraid to feel the climax I knew was rapidly approaching.

I came when he slid three fingers into me and flicked my clit with his tongue, all while he looked up at me with those impossibly sexy eyes of his. It was too much. I flattened myself against the table and I couldn't hold in the sounds any longer. Before, I'd been biting back the loudest of the moans threatening to escape from me, but now they all came free. I gasped, I writhed, and I eventually sat up to look at the man who was now upgraded from Sex Robot to Sex Magician, because there was nothing robotic about what just happened, and the way that slick tongue of his had made me instantly forget all the ways he had tried to piss me off over the past week was nothing short of magic.

My eyes wandered down his body to his erect cock, and I raised an eyebrow at him. And then the phone rang.

I expected him to ignore it, but Bruce glanced at his cell, which was sitting on the corner of the table, where he must've stripped it from his pocket before dropping his pants. He seemed to recognize the number on the ID and he actually snatched the phone up.

"What is it?" he asked.

I tried not to let my disappointment show. Until now, I'd felt like the only thing in the world that mattered to him. It was a good feeling. An *amazing* feeling. Then one simple act managed to undermine it all. I sat up and gathered my blouse, which was sitting beside me on the table, and held it in my lap, positioning my arms to cover my breasts as much as I could. He hadn't sent me away, but I immediately felt strange and silly for being naked, even as he stood there looking like a statue carved by a Greek master sculptor, completely naked and completely erect.

There was a pause while the person on the other line spoke. Bruce's eyes shifted to me in a way that wasn't entirely kind. It was the kind of way I thought you'd look at someone you were worried was eavesdropping.

"I can go," I said quickly.

Bruce hesitated. He looked at the phone again, eyebrows drawing down as he listened to whatever was being said. "Raincheck?" he asked.

My stomach felt like it dropped straight through me. I was mortified, embarrassed, and more than a little pissed off to be thrown out because of a phone call. Obviously, this didn't mean much to him, even if I had been busy trying to turn it into something significant in my own head. I didn't want him to see my disappointment. If he knew how much his dismissal stung, he'd know how much I had been willing to give up for him. At least this way I could pretend it was casual for me, too.

I got up as nonchalantly as I could and slid back into my bra, blouse, and skirt. I even snatched up the torn remains of my panties and tucked them into my purse before giving him a tight-lipped smile and leaving.

I could still feel where I was wet between my legs from his kisses and his tongue. I could feel the numb tingle in my lips where we'd kissed each other raw. But now, it all felt like just another taunt. Another teasing reminder by him that he owned me and I was nothing but a toy for him to cruelly bat around until he got bored.

I was suddenly glad I hadn't confessed the real reason for my internship, after all. Maybe it wouldn't be such a hit to my conscious when I found dirt on him and exposed it.

10

BRUCE

I told Natasha to take the day off, but I guess I shouldn't have been surprised when she was waiting in front of my apartment in the company car. She had her hair pulled up into a business-like bun, which *almost* made her look professional.

I leaned in the passenger window and reached to rub something purple and sticky from the corner of her mouth. I licked my finger and grinned. "Toast with jelly for breakfast?" I asked.

She cleared her throat while she rubbed at the spot. "I don't know how that got there. I must've bumped into someone's breakfast on my way out this morning."

"Of course." I pulled open the door and got in. "That's the most likely explanation, by a long shot. So, mind telling me why you aren't taking the day off like I asked?"

She gripped the steering wheel until her knuckles turned white and stared at the road. "Because I'm not going to let what happened last night in the office make things awkward. Whatever that was... it happened, and it doesn't matter *how* it happened. I'm still your intern and I'm going to do my job."

"Even if your job is putting up with my shit until you quit out of sheer frustration?"

She relaxed her grip on the wheel a little and grinned. "And how is that different than any other job?"

"Well, I'm not paying you, for starters."

"There is that," she admitted. "But internships are the new slavery. If you're under thirty and you want a job, you've got to be lucky or talented out of your mind to avoid them."

"Don't forget the forty and over crowd," I added. "They don't get hired either because they're more expensive than you young slaves, or we just assume they don't know how to work email."

She thought about that for a second. "I guess you picked just about the only way to make it in the world, didn't you? Become your own boss and make your own rules."

"Until you meet somebody who refuses to play by them," I said. I let my eyes linger on her long enough for her to understand my meaning.

She looked down, chewing her lip in a way that was quickly becoming my kryptonite. "Natasha... I'm sorry about last night."

She shook her head, quickly straightening and staring back at the road again. "You don't need to apologize. It's what it was. Sex is just sex, anyway, right?"

"Yeah," I said, even though it had felt like it was going to be a whole lot more than sex. It had felt like I was about to throw away all the precautions I'd been taking with my heart for the last two years, like I was going to dive in head first and say screw the consequences. But then I saw Valerie's number on my phone. She only ever called when something was wrong with Caitlyn, and I knew it was a call I needed to take.

"I'll be blunt," I said. "I asked you to stay home because I'm going to see my ex-girlfriend today. She was the one who called last night."

Natasha's face fell, but she was quick to smooth her expression back to neutral. "Okay. Where does she live?"

"Natasha," I said. "I can get my driver to do this. You don't have to—"

"I'm just your intern," she said. "Right? Why should I care if I have to drive you to see your ex?"

"I'm just saying you don't have to. You can take the day off."

"No," she said. She started the car and merged into traffic, and I was almost grateful that she didn't talk for the rest of the drive.

We parked just inside the north end of Tribeca. Natasha glanced around and then gave me a curious look. "Isn't this the part of the city where people like Leonardo Dicaprio live? Was your ex a movie star?"

"No," I said. It wasn't easy, but I kept the bitterness from my voice. "A waitress, actually."

The curiosity on Natasha's face deepened. "And she lives here?"

"Yes," I said.

"Okay, you win. I'm curious. Are you going to make me beg, or do I need to resort to blackmail? Don't think I've forgotten about the torn panties. Last I checked, destruction of personal property was a pretty big deal in a legal court."

Her words immediately brought me back to last night, and I felt the rush all over again. She had tasted so goddamn good, but the farther I got from what happened, the more it felt like it was the kind of experience we couldn't repeat. Valerie's call had come at the worst possible moment, and it felt like some kind of warning from the universe to avoid making the same mistake again.

Even though nothing about Natasha felt the same. Still, there were multiple paths to the same destination, and every path I'd ever started with a relationship or a commitment had lead to the same dead end.

"There's nothing to tell, really. I was stupid and thought she was into me. Turned out, she was into my bank accounts. Literally. I was the dumbass who decided we were far enough along to trust her, and once she'd taken as much as she wanted for herself, it was too late. I wasn't going to drag her into a legal battle because it'd mean dragging her daughter along for the ride."

"You have a daughter?" asked Natasha, who stopped walking suddenly and put her hand on my arm.

"No," I said. "Caitlyn was Valerie's daughter from a previous relationship. She'll be nine next month."

"And you let Valerie get away with robbing you to protect her daughter? Jesus," she said to herself. "You must really care about Caitlyn."

"She's a good kid, but no judge in his right mind would give me any kind of visitation rights." I chuckled, studying the ground as we walked. "To tell the truth, I think I had stopped feeling right about things with Valerie before I ever found out, but somehow I knew she'd take Caitlyn away if I ever broke things off. She was spiteful like that, and she knew how to get me where it hurt."

"I'm sorry. Is that what the phone call was about? Does she want more money?"

I was surprised again by how perceptive Natasha was. It was easy to see the pretty face and the fit body and think she was like so many women in this city—pretty on the outside and empty on the inside. She had a way of constantly reminding me she was far more than that, though. "More or less," I said.

"So she lives in Tribeca but she's still begging you for money?"

"You know what? Why don't you come inside when I go to see her. I think it'll be easier to understand if you see for yourself."

11

NATASHA

Valerie's apartment was massive. It was the penthouse suite in building that used to be some kind of industrial factory, which was true of most buildings in the area. At some point, a developer came along and gutted out most of the industrial buildings to turn them into what was basically the closest you could get to mansion-style living in downtown New York. I cringed to imagine how much Valerie must've stolen from Bruce to be able to afford a place like this.

Bruce looked so put together and clean as I followed him through the lobby of her building. It was impossible to stop picturing the perfect body under his suit and the way he had grinned while he was eating me out. The memory sent a hot shiver through me.

Time had only managed to make me more confused. On the one hand, I was still offended that he sent me away in the middle of what we were doing because of a phone call. At the very least, I deserved an explanation. He had to have known how self-conscious it made me to be sent away in the middle of the act like that, as if I'd done something wrong or soured him on the idea.

The bit of explanation I got as we walked from the car was a step in the right direction, but it still didn't feel like it was enough to put my mind at ease.

I had the piece for Hank to think about, and as the days drew on, I felt more of a desperation to get it moving in *any* direction. I'd originally figured just being around Bruce would be enough for something useful to leak my way, but I hadn't heard a word. Besides, every time my personal feelings got mixed up into the equation, I questioned whether I'd even be willing to go through with writing a piece that could hurt him. If I was being honest, I knew I couldn't, as things currently stood. But it was easier to keep going through the motions than face reality.

I didn't have a payday coming until I finished this piece, and quitting the piece would mean quitting as Bruce's intern. Writing the piece would mean cutting Bruce out of my life, too. I knew I wasn't ready to do that, but the clock was ticking. My bills weren't stopping any time soon, and before long, I was going to have to do something. But what was I supposed to do when I didn't like any of my options?

Bruce knocked on the door to Valerie's apartment and waited. I rocked on my heels and laughed a little nervously. "Wonder what she'll think when she sees me, huh?"

"If I know Valerie, you won't have to wonder for long."

The door opened to reveal a woman I assumed was Valerie. She was a little taller than me with hair dyed a platinum blonde from the looks of it. She was gorgeous, and I hated that the realization sent a spike of jealousy through me. I tried not to imagine her and Bruce together, or how I must've seemed so plain by comparison. She had the perfect, perky little pixie nose, lush lips, big eyes with thick, elegant eyelashes, and a wide forehead with a narrow chin that almost came to a point. She also looked like she probably had a personal trainer and never ate anything but vegetables and chicken.

She looked straight past Bruce to size me up. Her eyes moved from my feet to my hair and then flicked away. It was a cold dismissal. She had been assessing whether I was a threat or not, and had decided just as quickly that I wasn't. I'd never been the competitive, catty type, but part of me wanted to blurt out that I was more of a threat than she seemed to think since Bruce seemed to have a great time between my legs.

It was stupid though. Immature, even. I forced the thought down and tried to be an adult. She was his ex for a reason, and I didn't need to compete with her.

"Come on. The papers are in the kitchen," she said.

Bruce and I followed her, and I spotted a young girl lounging on the couch with big headphones on and a tablet in her hands. She must've been Caitlyn. I searched her features for similarities to Bruce for a few seconds before remembering she wasn't his. It was evident, too. Her biological father must've had some Latino blood in him, because Caitlyn looked like a budding, more exotic version of her mother with tanned skin and a beautiful auburn color in her hair.

Her eyes darted up when she saw Bruce, and her little face spread into a huge smile as she tossed off her headphones and ran to hug him. Bruce laughed as he pulled her up into a tight hug so they were ear to ear. "I missed you," he said quietly.

Valerie watched this with folded arms and a plainly annoyed expression.

"Why are you here?" she asked as he put her down. "Are you staying?"

"I'm sorry, bud," he said, kneeling to push her hair behind her ears. "Not this time."

I saw a different side of Bruce in those few, quick gestures and words. I saw his heartbreaking before my eyes, and I realized why the breakup had been so hard on him. He loved that little girl like his own daughter, and Valerie hadn't just ripped him away from her. She'd used her like a human shield between him and the justice he deserved to take.

Caitlyn lowered her eyes, but nodded.

"Come on," said Valerie. "I have an appointment in half an hour."

I expected Bruce to stand up to her or give her some of the sarcastic, biting remarks I'd come to expect from him, but he just followed her. It was hard seeing him like this. I guessed he must have known the leverage she held over him. It didn't matter if what she was doing was right or wrong. She held Caitlyn's well-being against his throat like a knife. If he gave her reason to, I could definitely picture Valerie doing something to hurt Caitlyn. Not physically, I thought, but something told me Valerie was more than capable of emotional warfare.

I tried to sneak a look at what it was Bruce was being forced to sign. It was a thick packet of documents and he was flipping from page to page, signing without more than cursory glances at the pages. Valerie only stood and watched with a kind of satisfied confidence. It wasn't the first time, I could tell, and she was so sure he'd do what she wanted that it made me want to punch her in her perfect little nose.

He signed the last page, set the pen down, and pushed the papers away before giving her a questioning look. "That all?" he asked.

"For now. See yourself out."

There was such a coldness between them that I found myself crossing my arms and fighting back shivers. Valerie walked off with high-heeled clicks on the expensive marble floors, leaving us to find our own way out.

When we turned to leave, I saw Caitlyn standing in the doorway with drawn eyebrows. "You don't have to let her do this to you, Bruce."

"I know," he said, brushing her cheek with his thumb and giving her a smile. "It's just money, though, bud. I have more than I need. If it keeps your mom happy and keeps you out of trouble, I don't mind it."

"I want to live with you," she blurted.

From Bruce's reaction, it wasn't the first time she'd brought this up. "Hey. I know it can be hard to understand her sometimes, but Valerie is your mom. She does love you in her own way." He lowered his voice and leaned a little closer. "I'd obviously adopt you in a heartbeat though, but I'd have almost no chance at all of getting you from your mom legally. If anything, I'd end up getting you yanked by child protective services, even if there was enough of a case for that, which I doubt there is, and then we'd have to hope I was allowed to be the one to adopt you from there."

"She doesn't even talk to me. She just gives me this stupid debit card with a ton of money on it and thinks she's the best mom in the world. I hate her."

"Hey," said Bruce. "Don't say that." He paused, and a grin spread slowly on his face. "Not so loud, at least."

Caitlyn smiled back at him, and it broke my heart seeing the two of them. No wonder Bruce was so guarded. Losing this little girl must have felt like having his heart ripped out and stomped on. His coldness was probably just a defense mechanism. No one could hurt you if you pushed everyone away, after all.

"Please try something," she said. "I don't care if I have to go to court or—"

"You're still here!" shouted Valerie from another room. "See. Yourself. Out."

I noticed the way she had pointedly denied my existence after her once-over of me, and I stashed that away as fuel for my desire to see the woman get what she deserved. I had no idea how I'd do it, but my dislike of Valerie had woken up a kind of protectiveness in me. It was strange to think of Bruce as someone who needed my protection in any sense of the word, but he had been hurt, and while he might still be a mega-star of the business world and in absolute control of his business, this was an area of his life where he wasn't on top. He'd been walked over.

Once he had given Caitlyn a quick hug goodbye and

promised to keep in touch, we made our way back to the street outside.

"I'm with Caitlyn," I said. "I hate her."

Bruce gave me a half-grin. Some of his normal self seemed to be creeping back in already, as if there was an aura over that place that drained all the fight out of him, but outside it could safely come back. "Want to get lunch before we go back to the office?" he asked suddenly.

I looked at him in surprise. "What, like a date?"

"Business meeting," he said quickly.

"You don't pay me and you don't let me do anything remotely important. I'm going to call it a date if you won't."

He grunted, but didn't argue the point.

Bruce managed to find a store with a banana that was up to his specifications on our way to a restaurant. He ate it as we walked.

I glanced down at the time on my phone. "Wow. We're at least half an hour past your normal banana time, Bruce. I don't know how you made it."

He gave me a dry look. "I have a routine I prefer to stick to, yes. But I'm capable of adapting."

"That's exactly what a robot would say."

We were seated for lunch a little while later. Bruce sat across from me at the small metal table, and we were given a tray of buttery, fluffy bread rolls and a simple salad bowl to split when the waitress brought our drinks.

I ordered water, because I didn't want a repeat of the last meal we'd shared where I got so drunk he had to carry me home. "I'm sorry, by the way," I said.

"For what? I can call up a pretty long list of things you've done wrong, so you'll need to be more specific."

"Very funny. But I'm sorry for today. It wasn't my place to butt in on your life like that. You tried to get me to stay home and I should've listened."

"I could've made you stay in the car. It was fine. For some reason, I wanted you to meet them."

"Honestly," I said. "Meeting them did help me to see why you're such an asshole all the time. I would be too, if I had to deal with that woman."

He nodded, and he still hadn't touched the bread, but he was serving some of the salad up on his plate. "I just hate that Caitlyn got stuck in the middle. She deserves so much better."

"She seems really sweet."

He nodded. "She plays piano, and she's really good at it. I still sneak into her recitals, but I probably don't need to bother with the hiding. I haven't seen Valerie at one in months."

"Was Valerie always... *that way?*"

"A cold-hearted bitch?" he asked. "No. She did a good job of making me look like an idiot for years. She had me convinced she cared about me and wanted a future together. I never knew if I had it in me to settle down and start a family, but Caitlyn was such a sweet kid. Valerie and I got along, even if there weren't sparks and fireworks when we touched or anything like that. It seemed good enough, I guess."

"And you've experienced that before?" I asked. "The sparks and fireworks thing?"

He studied his plate for a moment before lifting his eyes to mine. "Not at the time. No. I'd heard others talk about it but never felt it for myself. I had begun to think people were exaggerating."

"Until?" I prompted as my throat felt like it was rapidly drying out.

He leaned forward and lowered his voice to a low rasp. "Until I kissed you in the break room. *All over.*"

I shivered and took a long sip of my water. "I liked it, too."

"That's a ringing endorsement."

I chewed my lip and jabbed at the melting ice cubes with my straw. "I liked it a lot," I said quietly.

"Okay. You're blushing. I'll accept that."

I covered my eyes with my hands, but couldn't help peeking back out at him and sighing. "I swear. I'm not usually the blushing virgin type. You just have a talent for embarrassing me."

I chose that precise moment to bump my water and splash all the rolls and most of the tablecloth. I set my now-empty cup back upright and looked at the ceiling like I could expect some angel to come down and reverse time for me. Maybe they could go ahead and rewind about a week while they were at it.

Bruce didn't even flinch. "You know. I think that was the longest you've gone without some kind of act of supreme clumsiness since we've met. It has been at least half a day."

"And I think this is the most off your routine I've ever seen you," I added. "I think we're rubbing off on each other."

Bruce raised his eyebrows. "That could be arranged."

I didn't understand immediately, and when I did, I felt a rush of warmth. "What if I don't want to be your plaything?" I asked.

"Then you had better put in your resignation soon, because I can't promise I'll be able to keep my hands to myself after last night."

I CHECKED IN AT *BUSINESS INSIGHTS* AFTER BRUCE LET ME OFF EARLY for the day. It was my first time seeing Hank and Candace in close to a week, and it already felt strange being back here. More than anything, it was a reminder that I was failing miserably when it came to my actual job. I sidestepped most of Hank's questions about how things were going with Bruce and pretended I was making headway. Candace knew me too well for the same tricks to work.

"So?" she asked. "You getting dirt yet? Or are you just getting dirty."

I was leaning against her desk and she was twirling a lock of her short-cropped hair in her finger.

"Something might have happened. But now I'm having second thoughts."

"About what?"

"Everything. The piece I'm supposed to write. Whether or not there's even anything *to* write about. What the hell I'm doing having feelings for Bruce Chamberson? Should I go on?"

"Just ask Hank to reassign you if you're not feeling comfortable about the piece."

"And prove to him and everyone else that I deserve all the crappy assignments he has been giving me until now?"

"Is that your biggest concern with getting reassigned?"

I sighed. "No. It should be, but I'm more worried about the fact that I'd probably never see Bruce again."

"Then tell Hank there is no story. You wouldn't be failing. You just did your job and there was nothing to dig up."

"Maybe, but if he decides to send someone in after I give up the piece and they find something? I look even more incompetent."

"So... figure out if you are serious about Bruce or not. If you are, you give up the piece and you're back to where you started here, but you are poor and working crappy pieces with a billionaire boyfriend. Or, if you decide it's not going to work, you dig and dig until you find something nasty to write your piece about. There. Problem solved!"

I smiled. "You do make it sound pretty simple. But what happens if it won't work out and I still don't want to make him look bad because he's not as bad a guy as I thought?"

"Well, then you're just up shit creek, I guess. You give up the piece and you go back to how things were minus the sexy billionaire boyfriend?"

12

BRUCE

I had a routine. Exercise. Breakfast. Work. Banana. Lunch. Work. It had almost become a religion to me. I made life work around my routine, and not the other way around.

Natasha had been in my life for just over a week now, and she was already finding ways to change that. It was ten in the morning. In other words, it was banana time, and I wasn't at work and there wasn't a banana in my hand.

Instead, I was holding a dog's leash in the middle of Central Park. Natasha's dog, to be exact. I had recently learned the chubby little thing's name was Charlie. For some reason, Charlie had decided he liked me. I grudgingly scratched his wrinkly head while he sat by my leg.

We were watching as Natasha knelt by a guy maybe in his late twenties or thirties who was sleeping on a bench. He looked pretty worse for wear with a few day's stubble that didn't look like a fashion statement and stained clothes. The guy sat up, said a few things, and then hugged Natasha tight.

Apparently, he was her brother. She'd gotten a call and suddenly asked me to leave for a few hours in the middle of my workday. I pressed her for details, but all she'd tell me was that her brother needed her.

Oddly enough, coming with her hadn't felt like a choice. Natasha was accident prone and unlucky. She sometimes overlooked common sense in frightening ways, and the more I got to know her, the more I felt I needed to be by her side at all times just to keep her alive. But coming along didn't feel like it was just about that. I wanted to be there for her when I saw how upset she was.

I scratched Charlie's head while I worked through my thoughts. Somewhere along the way, I had stopped hating Natasha, I thought. I don't know when it happened or how. The idea of us in some kind of relationship was obviously ridiculous, but I'd slowly come to want to tease her instead of punish her. I liked the way she fired back when I poked fun at her. I liked the way she managed to carry so much sexual energy in the smallest facial expressions, and I especially enjoyed the fact that she had no idea how transparent she was.

She was dying to give herself to me again, and frankly, I was dying to take her. The only thing holding me back now was the confusion about what I really wanted. But why should I let that stop me? We were both adults. I'd made myself perfectly clear the other night after we shared the banana split. I didn't know where we were going and I wasn't going to make promises. All I knew was that I craved another taste of her.

I was also still paranoid about the possibility that any woman who showed interest in me was just another Valerie. They would play nice and put on a brilliant acting job until I made a fool of myself and fell for them. They'd sink their claws into me and my accounts inch by inch, and then once they had enough leverage, they'd snatch their share and leave me.

I could survive the frustration and the betrayal. I really could. Had it not been for Caitlyn, I would've been over Valerie in weeks, if not less. I would've given a law firm unlimited funds and made her regret she ever thought she could get the better of me.

What I couldn't stand was the idea that I was playing into someone's game.

I was a winner. It wasn't a point of pride or a source of cockiness. It was a business strategy, and it was one that bled over into my personal life.

Some people thought winning was about knowing a business or having talent. Others said it was hard work. I thought it was about self-discipline. Self-discipline had always been my talent. It was a weapon I spent time honing every day. Each time I worked out when I was tired or got out of bed before the sun rose. Every time I stayed late at work when I would rather be home. All the times I forced myself to stay focused and study instead of goofing off. Every single time made my self-discipline stronger, until it was a perfect tool I could use at will.

Except with Natasha.

She was an anomaly. It didn't matter how strong my will was. Eventually, the desire to have her and joke with her and *enjoy* her won out. I could fight it, and I could delay it, but I couldn't win.

"Here she comes," I said to Charlie, who was grunting in a way that was mildly disturbing as I rubbed behind his ears.

Natasha was holding her brother's shoulder like she was worried he might fall as she approached. "Braeden, this is Bruce. Bruce, this is Braeden."

I looked at his dirt-stained hand and extended my own for him to shake.

He took mine tentatively with the kind of grip that always made me want to cringe away, like his hand was a loose sack of blood with no bones in it. His eyes didn't leave the ground, and I read shame in his body language as clear as day.

"Do you need a place to stay?" I asked him.

"It's okay," said Natasha. "He's going to stay with me. *Right?*" she said tightly, nudging him.

"Yeah. I'll crash with you till mom and dad can come get me."

"Is there room in your apartment?" I asked.

"We make it work. It wouldn't be the first time."

"Nonsense," I said. "I have space at my place. It's two floors. The two of you can take the bottom floor and I'll take the top. At least until your parents are able to get you."

"It's really generous of you to offer, Bruce, but I don't see why you'd need me there, too," said Natasha.

I tried to quickly think up an answer other than the fact that I wanted her there and failed. "Well, my offer still stands. You want to stay at my place, Braeden? Free food and drinks. You'll enjoy yourself."

He looked up finally and gave me a reluctant smile. "Do you have wi-fi?"

I LET BRAEDEN BORROW SOME OF MY CLOTHES AND USE THE GUEST bedroom as his own. Natasha and I stood in the living room of my apartment while the water ran in the background.

"This really was nice of you. Thank you," she said.

"It's nothing. I'm hardly ever here, anyway. He won't be in my way."

Her forehead wrinkled up and she looked down, tugging at her arm like she was on the verge of some kind of big decision.

"What is it?" I asked.

She hesitated. "It's nothing. Hey," she said quickly. "You haven't had your banana yet. Do you want me to go get you one?"

"You think you can find one up to my standards?"

She rolled her eyes. "It's not rocket science. Do you want one or not?"

"Yes," I said. As if on cue, my stomach growled. The truth was that I already felt cranky without it.

Natasha left and I went behind where her brother had already moved things out of place. I nudged the ottoman back in line with the couch arm. I straightened the painting he moved when he bumped into the wall. I went in the fridge and made sure everything was where it was supposed to because I had offered him up whatever he wanted.

I didn't mind the straightening. It had always brought me a kind of calm. It was my form of meditation. I wondered if that was part of what made me enjoy being around Natasha so much. She gave me the ability to constantly have something to fix. I wasn't sure that was really it, though. It might have been simpler. Maybe I just enjoyed that she was genuine. She didn't try to suck up to me or sugar coat things. She was real with me, and it made me want to believe she really didn't have any ulterior motives.

She was a girl I could trust.

13

NATASHA

"You serious?" asked Braeden. We were in the guest room at Bruce's house. He had to head to the office for a meeting shortly after I brought the banana back, and he'd told me to take as much time as I needed before I came in. I had just finished explaining my assignment from Hank to Braeden.

"Yes. But it probably doesn't matter, anyway. I think Bruce is as clean as a whistle. And even if he wasn't, I'm thinking I couldn't write the piece. I wouldn't want to betray him."

"What if he finds out?"

"He won't. I'm only telling you because mom and dad know. I wasn't sure if they'd mention it to you and then you'd mention it to Bruce by accident. So you don't say anything about the piece to him, okay? I think I actually like the guy, and I don't want to mess it up. I need to find the right time to tell him myself, I guess."

"Yeah, yeah. I got it."

I looked at him and sighed. Thank God he had cleaned up. Seeing him the way he was in the park had broken my heart. "What were you thinking?" I asked. "Mom and Dad said you told them you were with me, but I didn't even have a text from you.

Did you think you'd just make it as a homeless man for a week or so until they were ready to let you back in the house?

He looked away and picked at the comforter on the bed he was sitting on. "I was thinking how shitty it was to keep putting you out like I do. I mean look at me, Nat. I'm a grown-ass man and I have jack shit to show for it. My crowning achievement is my pokemon collection, and yes, I realize how horribly pathetic that is. Mom and dad are sick of me. I know you'll never admit it, but I'm sure you are. *I'm* sick of me. I'm tired of being such a fuck-up, but it feels like it's too late to do anything about it."

I put my hand on his knee and squeezed. "Hey. You're not a fuck-up. You just haven't found your thing yet. Okay? So stop beating yourself up. And please don't ever think I'd rather find you sleeping in the park like a homeless person than deal with your mess in my place. You're a pain in the ass, but you're my pain in the ass. And I'm always going to be here to take care of you if you need it."

"Would this be a bad time to ask for a couple bucks?"

I fished out a five dollar bill I couldn't afford to part with and handed it to him. "Don't even tell me what this is for, but this is all I can afford right now. Bruce isn't even paying me."

"What?" asked Braeden, who pushed the bill back into my palm. "The guy lives in this fucking mansion and he's making you work for free?"

"It's an internship," I said.

"This is exactly why I'm chronically unemployed, you know. Let me guess, you're expected to just work there as long as they see fit and hope they toss you a job eventually?"

"I think that's the formula. It doesn't matter though. Not technically, anyway. I was only working at Galleon for the piece, remember?"

"Right. The piece you're too much of a softy to write."

"Even if I wasn't being a *softie,* I'm almost positive there is nothing to write about. He's just a guy who is good at what he does. He's not corrupt."

"Ah, the classic case of cock-goggles."

"First of all, ew. Second of all, I'm going to barf if I have to hear my brother talk about 'cock' again."

"Cock goggles," he continued matter-of-factly as if he hadn't even heard me, "are a widely-known phenomenon where a woman overlooks the fact that a man *is* a cock because he *has* a cock that she hopes to enjoy."

I stuck my fingers in my ears and fake gagged. "Please. Please. I'll give you my apartment if we can stop this conversation now and pretend it never happened."

"Tempting offer. Do all your unpaid bills come with the package?"

"Ass," I said. "Yes, they would."

"Then you can keep your shoebox and I'll keep being a failure. Sound like a deal?"

BRUCE'S SCHEDULE WAS FULL OF MEETINGS. BRAEDEN HAD ALREADY been staying at Bruce's place for three days now, and I'd admittedly found an excuse to come inside and check on my brother every day so far. It also gave me the opportunity to see Bruce out of his element. He was a little different at his apartment. Slightly less tense, but still the control freak I was coming to enjoy.

There were only five minutes left until he liked to have his banana, but he was still stuck in his meeting. I thought I'd do the helpful thing and bring it to him in the conference room, so I headed down to the break room. I picked up the banana, which had his name written in big black letters over almost every available surface.

"I see you're not afraid to touch the boss' banana anymore," said a woman's voice. I looked to the table in the break room. I thought I recognized her as the woman who had implied I was sleeping with Bruce a week or two ago. Thankfully, she was the only other person in the break room.

I held the banana up and looked at it, like it held the magical answer to diffuse the awkwardness. "Only with his permission," I said lightly, and then winced as I played my words back and found the innuendo. But it might have been possible to talk about a man's banana *without* innuendo.

"Oh, well it's nice that he asks you to do it first. You're still an intern though, so you must not be touching it right."

I considered walking away then. There was no point lowering myself to her level when she was clearly just trying to be nasty. It wouldn't been the right thing to do, maybe. But I didn't feel like doing the right thing, so I took a step toward her.

"You're really concerned about Bruce's sex life. Do you want me to tell him you're interested? He's in a meeting, but I'm heading in there now. I could let him know you're waiting in here for him. Would you like that?" I asked sweetly.

She pressed her lips together in an angry line as she stood and stormed out. I felt petty for stooping to her level, but I had to admit it was also satisfying. If she wanted to keep butting into my barely existent sex life and assume nasty things about me, she deserved it.

I opened the door to Bruce's meeting as quietly as I could, feeling more than a little self-conscious with the banana in my hand. There were serious looking men all around the table in expensive suits. Bruce was sitting next to William, which was still a jarring sight, like seeing him beside some kind of distorted reflection of himself from a dimension where he wasn't such a perfectionist.

Bruce eyed the banana, but William was the first to speak.

"Tell me, Bruce," said William. "Why is it that everytime I see your intern, she seems to have her hands on your banana?"

Bruce cleared his throat, and everyone in the room but William simultaneously shifted in discomfort.

"Sorry," I said. "I didn't want to interrupt but I knew you get cranky without this."

"You did a good job, Natasha." His eyes fell to my hand on the banana, and the way his eyebrow twitched up just a fraction of an inch managed to make me feel like I was doing something sexual as I handed it to him.

I straightened and smoothed the wrinkles from my skirt before nodding awkwardly to everyone, who was staring at me, and heading for the door. I gripped the handle and pulled but the door didn't budge. I made a sound between a nervous laugh and a grunt of desperation and pulled harder. I gave it three more firm tugs before I stepped back, huffed at the door, and then turned to look at Bruce with a helpless expression.

He got up, walked to the door, and *pushed*.

"Oh," I said. "Push, not pull, huh?" I scurried out of the room before anyone had a chance to say a word and then practically dove head-first into the nearest bathroom to decompress.

Bruce found me half an hour later when I was hiding by the copiers. I'd been "working" here for almost two weeks now and I didn't actually have any job responsibilities. It was maddening. I shuttled Bruce to and from the office. I followed him if he went on a business outing, but beyond that, I was forced to wander around the office and pretend I was busy.

One of the easiest things I'd found to do was to sneak a paper off someone's desk and make a bunch of copies of it. Then I could carry it around from one end of the office to the other until there was something to do.

It was ridiculous, and I knew Bruce knew, because I'd finally complained about it to him a few days ago. The smug bastard had just told me he liked seeing the "funny little ways" I came up to pretend I was busy.

"Hmm," I heard Bruce say as he walked up from behind me. "A hundred copies of somebody's order receipt for fiber pills from

Amazon. Yes. I can see why we would need to circulate that around the office."

I honestly hadn't even looked at what I was grabbing. "Tell me the truth," I said, ignoring his tease. "Did you guys talk about how much of an idiot I made out of myself in there once I left?"

He chuckled. "Yes. two billionaires from Japan and the entire executive staff of the biggest pharmaceutical company in the Western world sidelined their meeting to talk about the clumsy intern."

I glared at him, even though I felt a little relieved. "You don't have to be a sarcastic ass about it."

"I wasn't being sarcastic. They really did stop the meeting to talk about it. Mr. Kyoto was particularly amused."

"What?" I asked.

Bruce cracked a smile. "Now I'm messing with you. No one talked about it, Natasha. They hardly even noticed."

"I doubt that, but thank you. Look, Bruce, there's something I've been meaning to talk to you about."

"Me too," he said. He looked over his shoulder and saw a group of women coming toward the copier. "Come on. We can talk in my office."

Once we were in his office, Bruce turned, barely giving me any room between the door at my back and his body in front of me.

"I wanted to tell you—"

"Me first," he said, interrupting me.

There was no arguing with that tone. With those eyes. It was the same look I saw after he'd eaten the banana split, right before he ripped my clothes off and gave me the orgasm to end all orgasms.

"I'm done pretending I don't want this."

"This?" I asked breathlessly. "You're going to have to be more specific. You could be talking about a car you saw at a dealership. Or knowing you, a banana."

"You. I'm not going to fool myself anymore. I want you, Natasha. You make me want to be like I used to be. To let my guard down and enjoy life."

I swallowed hard. I needed to tell him. I wasn't going to even write the piece anymore, so how bad would it really be to admit the truth, that *yes*, I had originally come here to dig up dirt on him, but I decided very quickly not to do it. That counted for something, right?

My thoughts went back to the conversation we had after I met Valerie, about how he thought I was special because he could trust me.

He deserved to know the truth but I couldn't stop convincing myself there'd be a better time. Maybe an opportunity to tell the truth would come up where I'd feel he might understand. I was going to tell him. I knew I was. But maybe this just wasn't quite the right moment.

"What if I don't know what I want?" I asked.

"Then you can either spend the rest of your life wondering if it would've worked, or you can find out."

I felt that same feeling from the night we kissed, like the world was blurring out of existence around us. Everything about him seemed sharper and more intense. The full lips. The striking eyes. The crisp, clean smell of him.

"And what if we come to different conclusions?" I ask. "What if I decide I want it but you don't?"

"What if I'm tired of answering questions and I just want to taste you again?"

I let a smile play across my lips as I leaned in and kissed him. It was just as good as I remembered. Better, even. His tongue moved against mine slowly at first, but the kiss quickly turned from tentative and exploratory to hungry and desperate. He ran his hands through my hair, up my shirt, and down my skirt, greedily finding every last place he wanted and taking as much as he dared.

Our bodies grinded together. His erection pressed into me as he lifted me and held me against the door, kissing me and dry fucking me. I tried not to gasp or cry out like my body was wanting to. I knew his secretary was just outside the office and there could be any number of people waiting to come see him.

"You know," I said between kisses. "I think I owe you after last time."

"You don't owe me anything. I enjoyed it more than you did. I guarantee it."

He kissed my neck and my earlobe, lighting my body on fire with every touch. "Can't you just pretend you expect me to do it? Are you going to make me beg?"

"Do what?" he asked, pulling back slightly so I could see the wicked smile he wore.

"Return the favor," I said.

"You're going to have to be more specific."

Bastard. "A blowjob," I said.

"Hm. If you want to do it so badly, I suppose I wouldn't stop you."

I tried to swat at his face in frustration, but he caught my wrist, meeting my eyes with an intensity that made me feel like I was about to melt into a puddle at his feet. "Beg for it. Tell me how much you want my cock, and *maybe* I'll let you have it."

All my pride went out the window. This wasn't about degradation or self-respect. We were dealing in pleasure. It would turn him on to think I wanted to suck his cock so badly I'd get on my knees and beg if it came to it. When I looked at Bruce and the way he towered over me with those broad shoulders and perfect features, I wanted nothing more than to bring him pleasure. It was almost too hard to believe that a man like him was at my mercy, and the power from that thought was intoxicating.

"Please," I said, a little awkwardly. "Let me put your banana in my mouth one more time."

I thought he might grin or laugh, but he just took a step back and pressed down on my shoulders, urging me to my knees. When he didn't move to unzip his pants, I figured he expected me to. *He really must get turned on by the thought of me being desperately horny for him.* Good news for him, I *was* desperately horny, so I wasn't going to have to do a good acting job. I'd just need to let go and try not to let my brain get in the way of what my body wanted.

So I chewed my lip and shoved down every last inhibition I had. I let the pounding, unbearable desire to do every last dirty thing I'd ever fantasized about come to the surface, and I let it rule me.

14

BRUCE

She looked like a goddess at my feet. Big eyes, chestnut hair and gorgeous, big brown eyes. But my eyes couldn't leave her lips. Those full, perfect lips that were so made for mischief.

She leaned her head forward, and to my surprise, she pinned my zipper to her front teeth with her tongue in a seductive little pose and tried to pull it down. In classic Natasha fashion, it slipped out of her mouth. Her cheeks flushed red, which only made me even more turned on.

It was borderline insane, but I wasn't just crazy about the good parts of her—the way she had a good head on her shoulders and could surprise even seasoned businessmen with insightful thoughts or genius ideas, or the way she was kind and cared about everybody else before herself, or even the way she made me forget I was bitter and had spent most of my life building up walls to keep everyone out. Natasha had stumbled, tripped, and crashed her way through all my defenses in a perfectly choreographed merger of clumsiness and fate.

No, it wasn't just the good that drew me to her. I even loved the way she was a walking disaster. It was refreshing and endearing. The way she always seemed so adorably embarrassed afterwards was also a massive turn on, and right now, I thought I might just explode if she didn't hurry up and find a way to get my zipper down.

She clamped it between her teeth this time, leaving the tongue out of the picture, and managed to pull it down, even though her determination not to let the zipper go made it look more like she was grimacing than putting on a sexy show.

"You may have to use your hands for the button, unless you're exceptionally talented."

She arched an eyebrow up at me, and for a second, I thought she was actually going to try to undo the button of my pants with her mouth. Instead, she threw aside all the slow act and practically ripped my pants and boxers down. It was fucking hot, and if I hadn't already been fully erect since the first kiss, I thought I would've made it in record time to see how badly she seemed to want to do this.

She gripped the base of my cock with her hand, and even the simple touch made my body tense up. She looked up at me, letting those lips of hers curve into the mischievous smile I'd seen so many times as she stared down the length of my cock.

"Is this a bad time to say I've never done this before?"

"As long as you don't treat it like a banana and try to take a bite? No. It's not a bad time at all."

"You'll tell me if I'm doing it wrong?" she asked.

The sudden vulnerability was indescribably sexy. I shook my head. "Natasha. If your mouth is on my cock, there is no wrong way for you to do it. Trust me."

"I feel like you're underestimating my ability to screw this up."

"Just suck my cock," I said, grinning and pushing her head down until her lips were against me.

She was either lying about having never given a blowjob before, or she was a natural. I guess the third possibility is that I'd been teasing myself with the idea of fucking her for so long now that I probably could've gotten off to watching her reading a book.

I took a handful of her hair while she bobbed up and down on me. I didn't force her head down or thrust myself deeper into her. It was her first time, and I wanted her to be in control. At first, she focused entirely on taking me in her mouth. I could feel the tight ring her lips made as she moved her head up and down on me and the warm slickness of her tongue blanketing the base of my cock. Her hands were on my thighs, gripping tightly. I loved watching the way her forehead creased and wrinkled as she sucked me off, like she was enjoying this as much as I was and simultaneously surprised by that fact.

SHE PULLED ONE HAND FROM MY THIGH TO CIRCLE MY COCK JUST below her lips and started jerking me off while she sucked. The added friction made me throw my head back and clench my teeth. Fuck, she felt good, and I knew I would only last a little while longer if she kept this up.

I tormented myself more by craning my neck to look at her curves as she knelt and her skirt strained against her hips and ass. I could see a hint of her cleavage shaking freely with every pump of her fist on my cock, and then I had to squeeze my eyes shut to force myself not to fill her mouth with cum.

"Okay, okay," I said quickly. I didn't want to cum yet because I wanted to fuck her. It felt like I'd been waiting to get inside her from the moment I met her. I wanted to cum inside her, even if it was inside a condom, I needed it so badly it hurt. "You have to stop or I'm going to cum," I said again, a little more frantically this time.

She wasn't slowing down. If anything, it was like I was encouraging her.

"Natasha—*fuck*," I groaned. She was swirling her tongue around my cock now and using both hands on me. One was jerking me off and the other was massaging my balls. She was moving so fast now that I could hear the wet, messy sound of the blowjob, and it was possibly the sexiest sound I could've possibly imagined at that moment. It was raw and it was dirty. Thinking of prim little Natasha making those noises on my cock was the last straw.

My whole body tensed. My chest tightened and my eyes slammed shut. "I'm cumming," I gritted out. It was a final warning to let her avoid a mouthful of my cum but if anything, she pressed her lips tighter around me, like she was worried about losing even a drop.

My cock twitched again and again with each release of my orgasm, and to my surprise, she stayed right where she was.

Then when the last threads of my climax were fading to a dull, pleasant buzz, I realized she didn't know what to do. She was frozen on my cock, mouth probably full of my cum, and he eyes looked wide and slightly worried.

I barked a laugh. "This is where you either swallow or—"

She gulped, and raised her eyes to meet mine as she sat up and wiped her mouth with the back of her hand. "What was the second option?" she asked.

"Spit," I said. "But swallowing is a hell of a lot hotter."

She bit the corner of her lip. "So, how did I do?"

"Here's a universal tip. If a guy comes, you did perfect."

She grinned.

I reached to unbutton her blouse, because I may have already came, but I wasn't about to give up my chance to fuck her over a temporarily quenched sex drive.

She gripped my wrists and lowered her eyebrows. "What are you doing?" she asked.

"Taking off your clothes..."

"Why?" she asked, and then I saw the familiar hint of mischief twinkling in her eyes.

"Because I want to see every last inch of that perfect body when I spread you out and fuck you."

"What if I want to keep you waiting for a week like you kept me waiting?" she asked.

"Then I'd call it cruel and unusual punishment."

"Hm," she said, tapping her chin. She looked so sexy and fuckable at that moment, it was unfair. Her lips were still wet from sucking me off, and one of the buttons of her blouse was undone, letting me see the hint of her black bra. Her skirt was hiked up almost to her panties, too, as she sat on her knees, still right where she had been when she blew me. I'd never been tortured, but knowing she was about to tell me I couldn't fuck her had to be worse than anything a torturer could've dreamed up. "Call it cruel and unusual then," she said.

I couldn't quite believe my eyes when she stood up, fixed her blouse, and took a step back toward the door.

"You're serious?" I asked.

"I owed you a return of the favor from last week. Now we're even. Your move." She twinkled her fingers in a flirtatious wave before closing the door and leaving me speechless. I heard a loud thump and the raised voice of my secretary outside.

I quickly buttoned myself back up and opened the door to check on her. From the looks of it, she was getting back up after falling.

"Seriously?" I asked, but I beat my secretary to helping her up.

Natasha was blushing, but she waved me off once she was standing and tried to straighten herself up. "My leg was just a little bit asleep," she said quietly. "I was trying to stall before my dramatic exit but I knew that was my moment so I took it."

"You're unbelievable," I said.

I HAD ALMOST FORGOTTEN NATASHA'S BROTHER WAS STILL

crashing at my place when I got home. If it helped Natasha, I was fine letting him stay as long as he needed, but I honestly hadn't expected it to last more than a couple days.

Braeden was lounging on my couch in his boxers when I got home. I made a mental note to call the housekeepers later and tell them to pay special attention to that spot. He nodded to me.

"What's up, Bruce Wayne."

I frowned at him. "Is that the guy from Batman?"

"Is that the guy from Batman?" he asked incredulously. "What are you, thirty-years-old going on seventy? Yes, the guy from Batman."

I gestured to the fact that he was half naked on my couch. "That must make you thirty-years-old going on twelve?"

"Ha, ha," said Braeden. He popped what looked like a cheese puff in his mouth.

A fucking cheese puff? On my couch?

"Where did you get that?" I asked.

"Grocery store," he said, like I was an idiot.

"I have plenty of food here. Why are you wasting what little money you have on cheese puffs?"

"You call what you have here *food?* Maybe you can subsist on vegetables and chicken, but veggies give me gas and chicken grosses me out. I mean, have you ever seen that shit before it's cooked? Looks like they cut it straight out of an alien's ballsack."

I raised my eyebrows. "You're familiar with alien ballsacks, then?"

He tilted his head at me. "How do I know you're not the one with the weird fetish? Billionaire. Neat freak. Seemingly perfect? You're like a walking example of the prototype for a serial killer or a guy with a secret BDSM sex dungeon."

"Feel free to scour the place for clues while you continue being aggressively unemployed, if that's what you think."

"Aggressively unemployed my ass," muttered Braeden, who stood and faced me with all of his six feet of lanky, pasty self.

I looked down on him, literally and figuratively. "You realize most people would be kissing my ass for giving them a place to crash, right?"

"Yeah, well, most people wouldn't be dumb enough to wind up needing help from an asshole like you in the first place. So let's get that out of the way. You're not dealing with *most people* right now."

"Clearly," I said.

For a second, he looked like he was actually about to swing at me. Then he relaxed slightly and squinted his eyes at me. "What do you want with my sister, anyway? We can cut the shit before you try to make up some bullshit about this not being about her. This is all about her. You wouldn't be putting up with my obnoxious ass if you didn't want something from her."

"She works for me," I said simply. "A happy employee is a good employee. And with baggage like you? I think getting you out of her hair is a definite turn towards happy."

"Yeah, no shit. Why do you think I was hiding out in the park instead of bothering her?"

"Have you considered just getting a job?" I asked. "Stupid question, I know."

"You're right, it is. Me and the traditional kind of job just don't mesh. I'm a big idea guy." He tapped the side of his head. "I just need to keep at it until my luck improves, and I'll be good. Don't you worry about that."

"I wasn't going to worry. What about this. You take a job in my promotional department. Toss around some of those big ideas with the professionals. See if you're hot shit like you think you are."

"Fuck your charity," he said. Braeden shook his head and crossed his arms over his pudgy belly like I'd just asked him to shine my shoes with his personal toothbrush.

"Fine, I was—"

"Out of curiosity," he said quickly. "What would your charity job pay, exactly?"

"Nothing until you proved you were worth a damn. Get one of your big ideas pushed through into circulation with our promotional team, and then we can talk salary."

He chewed his nail. "Damn it. Fine. I'll do it, but you're still an asshole. I'm only doing this because maybe I could finally help Natasha pay the bills her shitty job can't."

I felt a pang of guilt at that. I wasn't paying her, after all. At first, I'd thought it was one of the reasons she'd have to quit. Then, when I got to know her better, I was afraid offering to pay her would actually *make* her quit. For a woman who needed money as badly as she did, she had a stubborn, prideful streak that I was sure wouldn't be receptive to charity. Still, I remembered all too well how her landlord had been trying to harass her about rent, and now her brother was mentioning her tight funds. I shouldn't have been surprised. New York was expensive, and I never quite understood how any but the top brass at companies managed to afford to live here.

A thought occurred to me for the first time. I left Braeden to taint my couch more while I opened up the laptop in my home office. I dug around in the company files until I found employee records. It didn't take me long to find Natasha. I wanted to know what job she'd worked before coming to intern at Galleon, if any. Had I actually interviewed her, I would've already known.

She had a waitressing job listed and a job in her campus bookstore, but that was it. I frowned. Based on the number of years she said she waitressed, that was supposedly how she had been paying her rent up until now. Something didn't sit well with that, so on a whim, I called up the restaurant she had listed and asked to speak to a manager. It took them a little digging, but they confirmed for me she had only worked there for two years, not the four she listed.

That left a two-year employment gap. A gap she was trying to cover up.

So what was her real job? And what kind of job would be so shitty that you'd try to cover it on your resume with a waitressing gig?

I spent some time trying to Google her name, but kept getting page after page of unrelated articles from some business magazine. I decided to stalk her social media next, not even sure what I was looking for, but overcome with curiosity nonetheless.

I found a post among her sparse Facebook activity mentioning how excited she was about a new job. The date was roughly two years ago. Heart pounding, I scrolled through the comments. Then I saw it.

· **Martha Flores:** Still can't believe my little girl is going to be a reporter! So proud!

A reporter?

I thought back to the articles I saw when I first searched her name and went back to click through the links. I realized they were articles written by Natasha Flores. My intern.

I sat back in my chair, head spinning and stomach dropping. She was a reporter. For a business magazine. And she hid that fact from her resume when she put in her application to be an intern for me.

It felt like Valerie all over again, except worse. Worse because I already cared more about Natasha than I think I ever cared about Valerie. Worse because I'd broken my number one rule. I'd made the same mistake twice.

"Yo," called Braeden through the door to my office. He punctuated his word with a heavy bang of his fist. "You have any toothpaste I can borrow?"

"Fuck off," I growled. I expected him to argue, but I must've sounded more pissed than I realized, because there was a slight pause with no sound and then I heard his footsteps retreating from the door.

I knew I should ask Natasha what was going on. It would've been the fair thing to do, but I also knew the threat of betrayal already stung so badly I wasn't thinking straight.

I texted Natasha and let her know I was going to be out of town tomorrow, so she could take the day off. Then I spent the rest of the night lying awake in bed, staring straight at the ceiling while the same icy rage I'd felt two years ago took me over. It was easier to remember now how I'd shut myself off from people. Natasha had started making me forget. I'd even started to think I had overreacted, that I should've just gotten over what happened with Valerie and moved on.

Now I remembered.

There was still a chance I was wrong. I knew that. But it was a small comfort. I'd always been a believer in following the simplest path to a conclusion. If all the evidence seems to point one way, that is the right way, more often than not. I even thought back on the times she'd seemed like she was trying to tell me something. Yes, maybe I'd been the one to cut her off, but she had more than enough opportunities to get the truth out.

I knew she had betrayed me. I knew it deep in my chest. All that was left now was to confirm it.

15

NATASHA

Bruce gave me the day off. I tried not to feel self-conscious about that. After all, I had just stepped way out of my comfort zone when I teased him about waiting a week for sex after I went down on him last night. If I had been completely honest, I was still scared to go all the way. I was worried I'd do it wrong or disappoint him somehow, and my little tease had been a cover I didn't think he'd accept. I had expected him to growl something at me, pin me to the wall, and take me anyway.

I couldn't be upset about it in the slightest. All Bruce had done was respect my wishes, even if I had stupidly hoped he wouldn't.

I was a coward, and I hated myself for it. I was hoping he'd do the heavy lifting for me. I wanted him to make all the choices and take over, but it wasn't fair. I was the one who needed to come clean about my real job. I'd decided forever ago not to write the piece—the piece which had no substance to begin with. It felt ridiculous. It should've been the easiest thing in the world to admit, but I'd dragged my feet for so long that the small lie had grown into something bigger, as small lies in close relationships tend to.

I resolved to tell him when he came back. I'd be ready for him to fire me or hate me, but I knew I needed to do it anyway. I couldn't keep stringing him along like this.

I headed to *Business Insights* to check in with Hank and Candace. I also needed to tell Hank I wasn't going to be doing the piece, after all.

When I arrived, Hank was standing behind his corner desk talking with a large, older man who was balding with liver spots on his head. It was Weinstead. I was staring at him in barely disguised shock when Candace rushed over to me and gave me a quick hug.

"Hey, stranger!" she said. She lowered her voice and made a conspiratorial face. "The bigwig is here. Dun dun dun..."

"Any idea why?" I asked. I'd only ever seen Mr. Weinstead once at a Christmas party.

"Oh I have a little bit of an idea. He was asking about *you*." She lowered her voice to do an impression of a grumpy old man. "Where's that girl doing the piece on the Chamberson brothers?"

"On the brothers?" I asked. "Hank told me it was just on Bruce."

Candace shrugged. "Alls I know is alls I heard."

I sighed. It wasn't like I was going to actually walk over there and introduce myself. I decided I'd just wait until Weinstead left. Then I could go talk to Hank privately and tell him the bad news. Accepting the fact that I was giving up on the piece felt like I was letting a part of myself go.

I was ashamed of how I hardly even dug for any real information about Bruce once I realized I had feelings for him. I felt like a silly little girl who didn't deserve to have a job in journalism. After all, I finally got a real assignment and I blew it. *Literally and figuratively.*

My heart stopped when Hank looked in my direction and his eyes lit up. He pointed at me, said something to Mr. Weinstead, and then they both started coming my way.

"Can I use you as a human shield?" I said to Candace, but when I turned to look for her, she was already fast-walking back to her desk.

Weinstead and Hank reached me with expectant smiles. Hank, for his part, looked like he was hoping I wouldn't embarrass him. Weinstead looked like he thought I was about to spill some of the juiciest dirt he'd ever heard on Bruce and his brother.

"So you're our undercover agent?" asked Weinstead. He had a kind of Santa Claus look, but a weirdly high-pitched voice and beady, dark eyes.

"You make it sound a lot fancier than it really is," I said, laughing nervously.

"Don't sell yourself short, Nat. You landed the job like it was nothing. Been imbedded over two weeks now. That's no chopped liver."

I forced a smile. "Well, it's not all that impressive."

"So," asked Weinstead. "Making progress, I assume?"

"I was actually wondering if you could give me any details on why you suspect the Chamberson brothers of corruption," I said.

"Let me give you a little tip from one journalist to another," said Weinstead. I noticed the look on Hank's face that seemed to say he was just as aware as I was that Weinstead had never even been close to a journalist, but did my best to look eager and receptive anyway. "Don't forget your job is to investigate the subject of your piece, not the person who assigned it to you."

I gave a tight-lipped smile. It was as clear a refusal to answer my question. "Well, I was only asking because I haven't seen even a hint of corruption in Galleon. Maybe if I stuck around for months, I would eventually overhear something, but even if I wanted to do that, which I don't, there's no way I could survive months without getting paid. The fee for the article wouldn't even come close to covering my expenses for that long a stretch, either."

Weinstead spread his hands and looked to Hank. "Then pay

the woman what she needs." He dug in his jacket pocket for a checkbook. "What do you need to stick on this case? Two thousand? Five?"

The casual way he threw out such staggering amounts of money as an option took my breath away. God knew I could use the money, but at the same time, this wasn't about a magazine piece anymore. It didn't matter how much I craved the recognition and respect that would come with a piece like this. Bruce was the subject, and there wasn't a price tag for smearing him or betraying his trust by playing along with this charade any longer.

"I'm sorry," I said. "I—"

That was the precise moment the universe decided to give me the worst case of bad timing in the history of my life. Just as I was reaching out to push the checkbook back to Mr. Weinstead, I saw Bruce Chamberson standing only a few feet away.

"You were supposed to be out of town," I said. I realized my hand was on the checkbook and snatched it back like I'd been caught stealing. "God, Bruce. I can explain all of this."

"You don't need to," he said, and it broke my heart when I heard the coldness in his voice. "You have bills to pay, and you were doing what you needed to pay them." He fished out a check from his jacket and handed it to me. "This is fair pay for the time you worked as my intern, including overtime. I had to ballpark some of the numbers, and I didn't include two hours of your time, because we weren't technically working."

Prickles of heat traveled across my skin at that. He was talking about the two times we let our desires turn to action, but the mention of those times didn't feel like it was intended as a flirtation. It felt like he was reminding me so I'd feel the fresh jab of how truly twisted it had been of me to fool around with him under these circumstances.

"Bruce, please..." I tried to give him the check back, but he folded my fingers around it.

"Take the money. But I don't ever want to see you again. Oh, and I prepaid for a hotel room your brother can use for the rest of the month. He already has the room key and knows where it is. I wish I could say I'll miss you. Goodbye, Natasha."

"I wasn't going to write it. Once I met you, I—I was going to tell you, but I was too scared you'd..." He was already walking away, showing no sign of hearing me or caring. I couldn't say which.

Mr. Weinstead slid his checkbook back into his jacket and fixed Hank with a glare. "I expect you'll find a way to rectify this? I need that piece."

"I'll do my best," said Hank.

And without another thought, the two men seemed to forget me. In an instant, I wasn't just back to where I'd started. I was lower. I'd had a taste of the possibility. The idea that one day I might climb myself out of the crummy hole I'd dug for myself in life. Instead, I'd fallen flat on my ass, right back at the bottom. Now Hank *knew* I couldn't be trusted with a real assignment. Worse, his boss knew. I was honestly going to be surprised if I even got the bottom of the barrel assignments going forward.

I tried to keep everything, and instead, I'd lost it all.

I SPENT TWO WEEKS FEELING SORRY FOR MYSELF. IT SEEMED FITTING. For two weeks, I'd lived a different life. A life where I tangled with the thrilling and scary idea of Bruce Chamberson and what a man like that could mean in my life. For two weeks, I'd known how fun it was to feel like everything I'd ever wanted was within reach.

So I spent two weeks purging it all from my brain. I tried to forget everything. Him. Galleon. *Business Insights.* I wanted to forget it all. I'd waited tables before, and the work might not have been fulfilling, but at least it was steady money. Maybe I'd need to find a place to live outside the city once my lease was up in a couple months, but I'd survive. I always had, and I would find a way now.

Braeden was visiting, which was a rare occurrence. He still had the room Bruce booked for him at the hotel, which felt like a weird thread to the part of my life I was busy trying to forget. Still, it was nice to see my brother because he felt like stopping by and not because he had to have a place to stay.

Despite his previous enthusiasm about not being a burden on me, my brother, as usual, hadn't changed a bit. He was laying on the floor by my wall, mostly because there wasn't room for a couch and I was already sitting on the bed.

"Think about it though," he said. "It'd be like a hammock but you could use it underwater. I mean, you can't seriously tell me that doesn't sound like a billion-dollar idea, can you?"

"Yes. I seriously can," I said a little more harshly than I meant to.

He sighed, sat up, and leaned his back against the wall while he scrutinized me. "You still bent up about Batman?"

You could say what you wanted about my brother, but he was a sweet guy. Calling Bruce "Batman" instead of his name was just one way he'd been trying to make me feel better, like we could make him into a big joke instead of the gaping hole in my heart he actually was.

"I'm getting over it, bit by bit," I said.

"You know. Not that I've watched too many romance movies, but isn't this supposed to be the part where the guy does all these grand gestures for forgiveness? You know, like the part everybody watching can splooge over because they get to see the guy down on his knees groveling?"

"Pretty much," I said. "The difference is, in those movies, it's usually the guy who royally screwed up. Not the girl."

"Okay, so why don't you take a cue from all the groveling men of the world. Do something grand. Make the guy forgive you. Somehow I don't think you're on a fast-track to impressing anyone like this, unless you're trying to out-do me in the whole unemployed department. But joke's on you, sis. Batman said I was 'aggressively' unemployed, and I don't think you'll ever top that level of praise."

I rolled my eyes, grinning. "No. You'll probably remain king of that one. But you seriously think he'd even care if I tried to apologize?"

"Would you, if the tables were turned?"

"Well, yeah. I'd care. I don't know if it would make a difference."

"Just because we like to wave our dicks around and flex in the mirror, it doesn't mean us guys don't have a soft side, Nat. Think about it. The poor dude just got out of one bad relationship and then he runs into you? He liked you, too, and he's probably embarrassed he let himself be seduced again by another wily woman who was out to get him."

I glared. "I was never out to get him. You know that."

"I do," agreed Braeden. "But does he?"

16

BRUCE

L ife went on, more or less. I'd woken up from a particularly enjoyable dream to a temporarily crushing disappointment to realize it was only fantasy more than once. Ever since I told Natasha to stay out of my life, it seemed that I had to remind myself she was gone every morning. She wouldn't be waiting in the progressively more beaten up company car in front of my apartment. We wouldn't have flirtatious exchanges on the drive to work. She wouldn't harass me about the fact that I wasn't paying her or that she had no real work to do.

She was gone. It was strange to me that in just a couple weeks, Natasha had made such a strong impact on my life that her absence could feel so staggering.

I knew I should be mad. Furious, even. I should be hurt. Maybe I was all those things to some degree, but nothing struck me as strongly as the feeling of loss. I knew I couldn't let myself go back to her, but I hated that reality.

So when I stepped outside my building that morning, I wasn't expecting to see Natasha. I definitely wasn't expecting her to be holding some god-awful ugly sort of quilt full of hand-sewn pockets.

"You don't have to say anything," she said seriously, apparently oblivious to the looks she was drawing from people walking to work. "But I'm sorry, and I know you love to organize things, so I made you something to keep your socks all sorted out. There's all these pockets, so you can put a pair in each pocket or just organize them by color..." her voice trailed off a little and she bit her lip. "I wasn't sure how many pairs of socks you have, but I could make you another if this doesn't look like enough pockets."

I took the thing from her and frowned at it. I was dying to say fuck it right there, to sweep her into my arms and kiss her, to tell her all was forgiven. But I had broken ties before she had a chance to make the wound as deep as it could have been. I'd gotten out, and forgiving her would be opening myself right back up for the dagger to the back I knew would inevitably come.

As much as I wanted to thank her and kiss her, I only took the blanket and walked to the car where my driver waited. I showed her the minimal respect of neatly folding it and setting it on my seat instead of tossing it thoughtlessly in the car, but I didn't dare give her more than that.

She was there every day after that, like a sad, homesick puppy. Sometimes she brought me coffee, and it never had sugar. She always brought a perfect banana. She even wrote my name all over it just like I had taken to doing once she ate mine by mistake that first day. I spent longer than I would've ever admitted sitting in my office, studying the girlish curves of her handwriting, as if they held some secret answer about whether this was true regret or just regret for being caught.

Most days, she said nothing. She just waited with the gifts and watched me with those big, innocent eyes when I took them. Every day, it was harder to resist. I had to force myself to say nothing, because I knew if I spoke, I'd risk saying what was in my heart instead of what was wise.

She made me so many handcrafted organization devices, decorations, and tools, that I started to wonder how she could

possibly think of anything else. After a few weeks, my apartment
was packed with things she had made me, most of which I found
surprisingly useful, especially the contraption she put together
out of hangers to hold all my ties in a way I could see without
having to flip through them. Of course, I'd already had a pretty
good system, but somehow, knowing Natasha had dreamed it up
made me instantly prefer her methods over mine every time.

I was a man of routine, and pretty soon, she became my
favorite part of my routine. I didn't wait all day for the banana I
had before lunch. I waited for the glimpse of her I'd get in the
morning.

The best gift she brought me was Caitlyn. It had been a few
weeks since she started the routine of waiting outside for me, but
she was holding Caitlyn's hand when I came out instead of something she'd made for me.

Caitlyn made an excited squeal when she saw me and rushed
to hug my legs. Natasha watched, even though she was trying to
make it look like she was studying the ground.

"How did you pull this off?" I asked. It was probably the most
I'd said to her since this whole thing started, and Natasha looked
surprised to hear me talking to her.

Caitlyn answered for her. "I'm taking journalism classes.
Natasha messaged me online and said she was a friend of yours,
that if I convinced my mom to hire her as a tutor, she'd bring me
over and we could hang out!"

"I'm pretty sure this is illegal," I said, but still hugged Caitlyn
back tightly.

"Well," said Natasha. "It's probably only just a little bit illegal,
if it is. But it's worth it, right?"

I got to meet with Caitlyn again the following Wednesday,
and Natasha said we'd do the same on Friday, but when Friday
morning came, Natasha was nowhere to be seen. I waited outside
for half an hour before I got worried. Natasha never quite grew
out of her tendency to be late for every reason under the sun, and

I figured she'd just missed a train or overslept, but I finally decided to call her.

It felt like a kind of surrender to reach out to her after all this time with her waiting outside my door, but I knew she deserved at least that much, if not far more by now. She had betrayed my trust, but she was going beyond what I thought just about any woman would to make amends for it.

She didn't pick up.

I tried her brother next, but he didn't pick up, either.

I called my secretary and check for an emergency contact in Natasha's file, wondering if I could possibly catch her parents somehow, but had no luck.

I had no choice left but to overreact, and I had my driver take me to the nearest hospital.

"Bruce?" said Natasha.

She was waiting in the lobby with red, puffy eyes. She rushed to me and hugged me tight. "It's Braeden. He got kicked out by my parents when his days in the hotel ran out, and he tried to sleep in the park again. He got in a fight and there was a lot of blood, but they're saying it might not be anything except a few lacerations on his scalp."

"Good. Your brother is an asshole, but I'm glad he's not dead."

Natasha laughed. "I'll make sure I tell him your exact wording on that."

I smirked, and it felt strange, like after the weeks of our strange, nearly silent dance, we had stepped into a moment of time where it was like nothing had ever happened.

"You know," I said after a moment. "If somebody really wanted me to forgive them. You'd think they would remember how much I enjoyed it the last time they got me a banana split."

Excitement flashed in her eyes. "Maybe somebody didn't think they would be able to pull the same move twice."

"Then somebody underestimated how much I love banana splits."

"Are you telling me I could've saved all the theatrics and gotten you to forgive me with a banana split from the start?"

"No. I'm saying you're adorably persistent, and I already didn't want to be pissed at you from the start, so you've done enough, and now I am just hungry for dessert before I forgive you."

"And you tell me this now, when I am stuck in the hospital worrying about my brother?" "Your brother sat half-naked on every conceivable surface of my apartment, moved my things around, and left a stench I haven't been able to completely remove. But if you want to make sure he's alive before we get dessert, I can respect that."

She leaned into me, forehead resting on my chest and let out a long, shuddering breath. "You mean it?"

"Yes. I don't know how your parents raised him, but he has no manners. It was unbelievable."

"No, you big idiot," she said with a small laugh. "You really mean you'll forgive me after what I did?"

"I'll enjoy having an excuse to be a hardass on you again. You'll need to accept that for now."

She nodded. "Gladly."

I sat across from Natasha in a trendy little cafe a few blocks away from the hospital. A banana split was between us, and I was digging into it like I hadn't eaten in weeks.

"Did you forget how to find your lunch without your trusty intern or what?" she asked.

I tried to slow down a little as I laughed at myself. "Well, you could say I've been a little distracted."

"By?"

"Remember the part where I said I'd enjoy being a hardass again?"

"Yes..."

"It means you don't get to ask the questions here. *Reporter.*"

She cringed at that, as if she wasn't quite ready to forgive herself for everything that happened, even if I was.

"Bruce, I—"

I held up my palm. "You don't need to explain. I've got an apartment full of shit you made for me with your bare hands. I've got weeks of proof that you're willing to do whatever it takes to prove you hate how this turned out. Call me simple, but I've got enough. Really, there's only one thing I still want."

Her eyebrows crept up as I let my gaze linger on her lips. I wondered what she thought I was going to say I wanted. *Her.* A kiss. A night with her alone. Another chance. I wanted all of those things, but I couldn't make myself say it, not yet.

"The banana split," I said. "I want the last bite."

I almost laughed out loud when I saw how much she deflated.

"What?" I asked. "Were you hoping I was going to say something else?"

"Nope. I just wanted that last bite, too." She was lying out of her teeth, but so was I, so I let it slide. This wasn't the kind of lying that shook the foundations of a relationship. It was the kind of lying that hid happy secrets.

I scooped it up on my spoon and then leaned forward so I could reach across the table to hold it at her lips. "Open up, intern," I said.

She gave me a wicked little smile and parted her lips to take the bite. I couldn't help remembering the way her lips had looked just as good when they were wrapped around my cock, and my heart rate quickened at the memory. What was it about dessert that got me so goddamn horny?

"You know," she said when she swallowed the last of the bite. "They say you know a guy is the one when he gives you the last bite of his favorite meal."

"Is that right?"

"It's what they say. But I say you know he's the one when you want him so badly you'll embarrass yourself for weeks on end just for the slightest chance of winning him back."

"Winning me, now, are you? Make no mistake about it, Natasha. You're the prize here. You always were. The only question was whether the price of taking you for myself was too high or not."

"So you're saying you only wanted me if I was cheap?"

"I only wanted you if I thought you wouldn't make a fool out of me. Over the last few weeks, I think I've come to realize I want you either way. Whether you make me into a fool or not. I just want you."

"That sounded dangerously close to something a sweet, thoughtful man would say. What have you done with the cold, calculating Bruce I know?"

"Maybe I'm only saying nice things so that you'll go to bed with me." I felt my own breath catch a little after I had time to digest my own words. Then I felt my heartbeat race when a slow, seductive smile spread across her lips. So much for happy secrets.

"Maybe it's working. But you made me wait weeks for this little date, I think the least you could do is show me a good time before you try to get me to bed."

"What, like a date night?" I asked.

"Exactly like a date night."

"Remind me when the tables turned again? Just yesterday, you were the one waiting outside my apartment, now you're making demands?"

She pressed her lips together, looked up, and then nodded. "Hmm. Yep. That sounds right."

17

NATASHA

Bruce took me to an abandoned theater near the edge of downtown. From outside, it looked like a huge concrete shell. We walked past the front doors, which were covered by chains, and headed around the side of the building.

"You're sure we're allowed to do this?" I asked for the fifth time.

"Stop being a worrier," he said.

"That means we're breaking in, doesn't it? When I asked for a date night I was thinking more like ice skating or ice cream cones."

"We just had a banana split, and you're already thinking of ice cream?" he laughed.

"*You* had a banana split. I think that last bite you gave me might've been the only bite I got."

He stopped and turned to grin at me, and *God* was he handsome. His hair was neat and pushed away from his face, but the hard, masculine lines of his jaw and fullness of his lips made a perfect fit to the buttoned-up look he wore so well. He just *looked* like success in his crisp white button-down and navy blue tie. He wore matching blue slacks that fit him deliciously snug around the ass and thighs. I still couldn't quite believe he was interested in me, even if I had done my best to screw it up.

"Maybe I wanted to make sure you were still hungry for my banana later."

I gave a wry smile. "If your goal was to get me to bite you down there because I'm ravenously hungry, then you're on the right track."

He winced a little. "Point taken. We can include a little ice cream on our date night, as soon as we're done with the creepy abandoned theater."

"Right. About that," I said. "Mind taking me behind the brain of the genius here? Is this just another way to punish me, or is there something I'm missing here?"

"Yeah. This was one of my favorite places when I was a kid. Before they closed it down, at least."

He yanked on a side door. To my surprise, it opened up. Sections of the ceiling were missing, which let dusty rays of sunlight stream inside to light the rows of cushioned seats and the damaged stage. A patch of the seats in the back corner were overgrown with moss and weeds, but some of the building was surprisingly well preserved.

I looked around at the faded murals on the walls and the shocking amount of decor that was left behind to rot until someone would eventually come to demolish the building.

He wiped off a seat near where we came in and motioned for me to sit. He sat down beside me and kicked up his feet.

"I'm surprised you can stand it in here," I said. "I'd think it would trigger all your compulsive need to organize and clean."

"Dirty things never really bothered me too much. I just like everything to be in order."

"You said this was your favorite place when you were a kid? I'm not sure I can picture you enjoying plays. No offense."

"None taken. I enjoyed it because we could never afford to see a show. My parents would use that door over there during intermission and we'd sneak in to watch the second half of the performance. Never the first half. I always enjoyed trying to piece together what had happened before. It was like a mystery.

"In some convoluted way," he continued. "I think the experience was part of the basis for my marketing philosophy. So many marketers want to tell you what a product can do. And me? I've always thought it was more effective to trick people into *imagining* what the product can do. The things we make up are so much better than the truth. I learned that here."

I narrowed my eyes at him. "I feel like you're trying to send me some deeply coded message and..." I waved a hand over the top of my head. "Woosh."

He smiled down at his lap in a rare moment of vulnerability. "No deep messages. I just thought of this place when I tried to figure out where to take you. It was always important to me, and it feels like a piece of who I am, I guess. I wanted you to see that."

I sucked my lower lip into my mouth and smiled. "I like that you wanted to bring me here." I leaned over to him and planted a kiss on his lips. He seemed surprised, but that didn't stop him from threading his fingers through my hair and kissing me back in a way that made me curl my toes.

I pulled back. "What if we go somewhere important to me next?"

"I'd like that."

WE SAT ON A BENCH IN THE SUBWAY WHILE PEOPLE WAITED FOR THE next train. Bruce gave me a curious look when he saw I was wanting to sit instead of taking a train to go somewhere.

"Here?" he asked.

"What? You're the only one who gets to have some kind of edgy special place?"

He laughed. "No. Though I wasn't trying to be edgy."

I gave a crooked smile. "Yeah. Me neither. This was just where

I fell in love with New York City. My parents always lived in New York, but not in the city. We'd come every couple years for a daycation, but never more than that, because the crowds always stressed my parents.

"One year, I got separated from them while we were taking the subway. They didn't realize I wasn't watching them and they got off the train without me. I ended up getting off once I realized they were gone and this was where I waited. It was before cell phones were so common, and they had no way to get in touch with me. I think they spent like eight hours trying to find me, and I just sat here the whole time.

"I remember watching everyone coming and going. I spent forever playing the game of guessing what they did for a living and what their lives were like. That was when I decided I wanted to be a reporter and that I wanted to do it while living here. It felt exotic and exciting. Like something out of a movie. Of course, ten-year-old me didn't know that a closet in New York City cost as much to rent as a four-bedroom house just about anywhere else. Still, I'm going to miss it here if I have to leave."

"Why would you need to leave?" he asked.

"Well, the money you gave me helped, but right now I'm waiting tables at night and trying to find another job during the day. After I make my morning visit outside your apartment, that is," I added with a growing heat in my cheeks. I still couldn't believe I'd taken my brother's advice on that, of all people, but he had been right to some extent. Whether Bruce was going to forgive me or not, it had felt good to make some kind of grand gesture of apology, like a kind of penance.

"Let me take a wild guess. I'm not allowed to give you enough money to help you stay?"

"Correct. Being a charity case never factored into my dream of making it in New York City. It's a prize I want to earn for myself, even if I do appreciate the offer."

He nodded, like he already knew as much.

"I know you paid some of my rent, by the way," I said.

He gave me a grudging nod.

"It was really sweet of you. It doesn't matter if my rent is probably pocket change to you. You were considerate when you thought I wasn't paying attention, even when you supposedly hated me and wanted me to quit."

"Yeah, well, don't tell my brother. He'll never let me hear the end of it if he figures out he was right all along."

OUR NIGHT ENDED AT A ROOFTOP RESTAURANT. STRING LIGHTS were strapped to the balconies and dangling overhead while heating lamps kept most of the chill out of the air. Bruce wouldn't admit it, but I was fairly sure he somehow managed to buy out the entire roof's seating, because we were completely alone while the interior section of the restaurant was packed.

The waiter came to take our drink orders, and I tried to order water because I knew there was no way I could afford anything here.

"She'll take your best wine," said Bruce. He held up a hand to stop my protest before I could mouth a word of it. "The most expensive, delicious thing you can find," he added with a grin.

"Is there a word for someone who's nice but is an asshole about it?" I asked once the waiter had left.

"A nicehole?" suggested Bruce.

"Yes. You're a nicehole."

"Well, you can be stubborn about not accepting handouts, but I'm old-fashioned. You come on a date with me, and I get to pay. It makes me happy to do it, so I won't accept any complaints."

I could've definitely felt guilty for accepting the offer if he had proposed it any differently, but Bruce had a way of making me feel like he really did enjoy treating me to the meal. It didn't feel like a handout. It just felt kind.

"Well, thank you, even if you're an ass about it, you're a nice ass."

"Did you just say I have a nice ass?" he asked.

"I actually never got a clear look at it when I had you naked, so I'm not positive yet. Why do you think I tried so hard to get you to forgive me?"

He barked a laugh. His smiles came so much easier now than when we first met, and I found myself wanting more of them every time I saw how good they looked on him. "It makes more sense now. First I thought you were after my money. Then my career. Now I realize you just wanted my ass the whole time."

"Precisely," I said.

The waiter came with a large, fluted glass the size of a vase and started uncorking and pouring the wine into it. The fluted tip of the glass made the wine spread evenly across the mouth of the bottle and cover almost the entirety of the glass as it filtered down to the bottom.

"Why is he pouring it into that thing?" I asked, quietly leaning forward so the waiter wouldn't hear my question.

"It's a decanter," explained Bruce. "It's how you know you ordered a fancy wine. Supposedly it helps with the taste. Something about aerating the wine. Bubbles and all that. To tell the truth, it all tastes the same to me. I'd usually prefer lemon water, but sometimes, when you're trying to get a girl into bed, you have to bring out the decanter."

"Is that right?" I asked.

"Definitely."

"And is that something you regularly do? Try to get girls into bed?"

The smile on his face melted away. "No. Not for a long time now, to tell the truth. I wasn't lying when I said I pride myself on only making mistakes one time. Valerie taught me how big a mistake it could be to give any part of myself to a woman. After her, I just kind of stopped. William would occasionally try to play wingman and set me up with somebody, but it never went anywhere. I felt too cold and distant, like the real me was watching and controlling my body from far away."

"Sex robot," I said. "Minus the sex, I guess."

"Yeah, like a robot. And definitely minus the sex part. Until you, at least."

"What about after me?" I asked. It was a nosy, needy question, and I hated that I felt compelled to ask, but it came out before I could stop it.

"After you? There was you."

I raised my eyebrows. "So you used me as a rebound girl for... *me?*"

"As of today, yes. You could say that."

"Hmm. I approve of that. If you're going to bang anyone to forget about me, I guess you couldn't do much better than me."

"So the whole 'banging' thing is confirmed then, is it?"

"You did bring out the decanter."

He eyed the decanter. "Yes I did. Hopefully this is the kind of expensive wine that costs a lot of money because it tastes good and not because some collector somewhere would blow his load to know how old it is and what vineyard it came from."

"I can see how that would be a common problem with ultra-expensive wines."

"It really is."

"So," I asked. "Is this a fish eggs and snail eyes kind of place, or do they have food I'd recognize?"

"It's the kind of place that probably puts an entire stick of butter in every step of the cooking process, but can make a bite of broccoli taste like heaven. Order this," he said, tapping a menu item I could barely read, let alone pronounce. "It's just a fancy word for super expensive steak that tastes really good."

"I'll trust you on that."

Whether I could pronounce it or not, the steak was so good I actually wondered for a moment if whatever the rest of the night had in store could possibly top it. It was that good. I'd spent weeks waking up in a hot sweat after dreaming about the things I wished I'd done with Bruce when I had the chance and now? I was pretty sure I'd be dreaming about vegan cows who lived a pampered lifestyle and probably got facials in the morning to make sure their meat was so tender it melted like butter in your mouth.

"I'm sure this cow had a great personality," I said once I swallowed a bite of the steak. "But wow. If you taste this good, there's no way you're not going to end up getting eaten."

"Maybe they died of natural causes," said Bruce.

"Or at the very least, I hope they got to watch *Pride and Prejudice* and *Terminator 2*."

Bruce screwed up his face and then laughed. "Uh, that's a pretty strange combination."

"Sometimes you're in the mood to gush and sometimes you're in the mood to watch someone get their ass handed to them. I think these cows deserved to have the best of both of those worlds before they died."

"I'm sorry to say it, but something tells me they died without ever seeing either movie."

I sighed, then took another bite and couldn't help making a soft moaning noise of enjoyment. "Well then I'm going to just have to settle for enjoying this and not thinking about it." I took a sip of the wine, which, by my amateur opinion, must've been the expensive kind that was expensive because it tasted good. "At least I don't have to feel bad about the grapes that died to make this taste so amazing."

"Cheers to that," he said, eyes twinkling as he raised his glass and gently tapped mine. I liked the way he looked at me. I could get addicted to it, in fact. It was the way men were supposed to look at women they cared about, but it was more than that. Yes, there was the almost adoring glint in his eyes, but there was something fun and dirty there, too. I could feel his want practically radiating across the table.

I didn't know if it was the wine or the food or the atmosphere. Maybe it was just Bruce. Whatever it was, a pleasant heat was swirling around in my lower stomach, and I was pretty sure my body was sending me about as clear a signal as a body can send with one message: *Sleep with him.*

There was only one hangup. One little checkbox that still didn't have a green mark through it.

"Bruce," I said quietly. "I need you to know that once I got to know you, I was never going to go through with writing the story."

"It's okay," he said. "It doesn't matter anymore."

"No," I said firmly. "It does. I may not have been planning to write the story, but I let the lie go on way longer than I should have. I should've told you the moment I knew I liked you, but I was scared the ride would come to a stop. The security guards would come out and drag me out of the theme park, kicking and screaming, and I'd spend the rest of my life wishing I could've stayed even another minute."

One of his eyebrows flicked up. "Unfortunately, we never technically got to the whole 'riding' part," he said.

"Can you take this seriously?" I asked, even though I couldn't help laughing a little. "I'm trying to put my soul at ease here and all you can do is make sex jokes?"

"You have my full attention."

"I'm just trying to say I'm sorry, but not because I was planning to sneakily gather dirt on you and write the story. I want you to know that was never my intention even after the first couple days. I'm just sorry I didn't tell you why I was there in the first place sooner."

"I can't be upset with you for not trusting me. I didn't trust you at first, either, so I'd say we're even."

After dinner, we went back to Bruce's place, and it felt

completely different going inside his apartment without knowing Braeden was there. I couldn't pretend I was there for my brother this time, and there was no doubting where the night was going.

Thankfully, Braeden was doing fine. I'd called several times since leaving the hospital to see if he was ready for us to come visit him and he kept telling me he'd kick my ass if I left my "dream day" with Batman.

All the excuses were out of the way. All the doubts had been laid to rest. Tonight was ours, and we both knew where we wanted it to go.

I felt it fluttering in my chest and pounding in my head as Bruce took me by the hand and led me through his apartment, straight to his bedroom. We both knew the flirtation and the waiting was over now. He'd played my game and taken me out for the night of my life, but it was time for the final act.

I was so nervous I could feel my hands shaking. Nervous for what, I wasn't sure. A new beginning. A possible ending. Or maybe just simply being disappointing to him somehow.

In his bedroom, I burst out laughing when I saw a banana sitting on his nightstand. "You have to be kidding me," I laughed, tears stinging my eyes.

"It's not what it looks like," he said.

I laughed even harder. "Oh God. I didn't even think about that."

Bruce was laughing now too, but he seemed to be having more fun watching my amusement than anything else. "Sometimes I wake up hungry, okay?"

"Okay," I said. I threaded my fingertips together behind his head, resting my forearms on his shoulders. Our eyes met, and the laughter dissolved into something heavier. Something full of pent-up desire. "My stomach is so full it hurts, but I'm already hungry."

He lifted me, pressing me to his chest as he walked me to the bed and actually threw me on it like I was as light as a feather. I landed on my back, eyes never leaving his. He looked down at me with unmasked anticipation.

"I've been waiting to spread you out and fuck you since the day I saw you. Since before I was ready to admit it."

I licked my lips as I scooted back to try to find the pillows, but I misjudged where I was on the bed and planted my hand over the side of the bed, nearly toppling over the edge.

Bruce was there before I could fall, and he slid me back into the center of the bed. "Can I trust you not to fall off while I take off my clothes?" he asked.

I blushed. "I'll do my best. But, maybe you should be the one to undress me, you know, since I might end up hurting myself somehow."

"Is that right?" he asked. He was leaning over me with his hands planted on either side of my head. He raised one hand to strip away his tie and toss it to the floor. He flicked open a few of the buttons on his shirt before he seemed to lose patience with it and focused on me.

I hadn't exactly dressed for a date night and sex with a gorgeous billionaire when I got ready in the morning. I'd dressed for day number five million of my groveling act—which happened to be a white romper with a floral pattern.

Bruce frowned down at it. "How do you get this thing off?" He started yanking at the waistband, which was nothing but a cinched up cord to keep it form-fitting. His touch on my waist tickled and surprised me, summoning up a bout of laughter.

"S-s-stop," I laughed. "Not there," was all I could manage.

I slid one arm out of the strap so he'd understand what to do next. He eased the next strap off my shoulder and then yanked the whole thing down, lifting my ass and feet to strip it completely off.

I took a quick glance down to remember what underwear I was wearing and crossed my fingers that I hadn't worn something too old. Thankfully, I was wearing pink, lacy panties and a matching bra. Given my usual luck, it was a miracle.

He licked his lips as he took in the sight of me, and he seemed torn between diving straight into kissing my body or stripping away the last of my clothes. A moment later, he bent his neck to kiss my chest and down along my cleavage and then the line down my navel to my thighs. Every kiss was an explosion of warmth and tingling nerves, like little ripples of pleasure that spread through my entire body.

I pawed at him with no shame, squeezing his muscles through his shirt and sliding my hands in the open seam of his shirt to feel his firm chest, gripping his biceps as he seemed to kiss his way across every last inch of me.

He finally made his way back up to my mouth, where he kissed me deeply, and then I felt his hand moving up my thigh. He let the side of his hand brush against me, drawing out a shiver that ran through me like a shockwave. I bit his lip a little harder than I intended, but if he minded, he showed no sign of it.

He dipped his hand into my panties, curling his fingers to reach me. My forehead scrunched together and my mouth hung open like I was in shock as he set his talented fingers to work. He slid them inside me to gather my wetness and then rubbed it up and down my pussy until I thought I was going to scream from the pure ecstasy.

I distantly thought I should probably be reaching for his cock to return the favor as he fingered me, but I didn't think I would be able to reach. Besides, he didn't seem to mind the way things were going at all if the way he was breathing hot over my neck was any indication. His body moved in pace with his fingers, softly grinding against me like he couldn't hold himself back until he was done, and his eagerness was a turn on in itself.

I'd never had much confidence, especially in the sex department, so every shred of excitement and horniness he showed me was like liquid encouragement that I drank up thirstily.

I held the back of his neck, not able to keep my fingers from digging into his skin and pressing his face into my neck. He felt so good, and he never stopped stealing kisses wherever he could reach.

His pace increased and increased until I thought I was going to cum. "I want all of you," I gasped. "Please. I want every inch inside me. I want to feel it."

He made a groaning sound, like my words were invisible hands that had started stroking him. He straightened and actually ripped his shirt open, popping off a button or two in the process. It was so out of character with his deliberate, organized nature that it sent a shiver of lust cascading through me.

He rolled to his back and worked his pants and underwear off, showing no effort to worry about some kind of sexy striptease. Bruce just wanted to get naked and get inside me as fast as he could, and I thanked God for that, because I knew I couldn't wait much longer before I would embarrass myself by literally ripping his clothes off myself and mounting him if he had delayed.

He dug out a condom from his pants and tore the wrapper open, sliding it on himself. I was relieved that he was thinking straight, because I wasn't sure I would've even remembered a condom right away. I might have actually let him inside me before the thought occurred to me, which was a little scary. I'd always been sensible. I'd always known I'd never let a guy near me without protection, and yet Bruce seemed somehow above those rules.

I sat up and reached for him, halfway pulling him on top of me even as he moved into place. His erection was poised between us, and I craned my neck to watch. I expected him to grip himself and guide it in me, but he just expertly rocked his hips, driving the head of his cock between my folds and spreading my slick arousal over himself for a few tantalizing seconds. Then, once he seemed sure he was ready, he guided himself in.

It wasn't rough, but it wasn't tentative. He started pressing himself inside me a bit at a time. My walls had to stretch to accommodate him, which definitely had not been the case the one time I'd slept with a guy before. I found myself liking the sensation, like I was being filled in a way I never realized I craved so deeply.

"Deeper," I gasped. "*God.* I want more. Please."

He made another groaning sound, leaving no doubt that he loved when I talked like that. I wasn't "talking dirty" for show or because I thought it was something he wanted. The words were just coming out of me. I had as little control over it as I might have over a sneeze. I'd never felt anything like it. It was as if my desperation for this was so intense that my body was overriding my brain and my self-consciousness.

"You'll get it all, intern. Don't worry." His words were a sensual rasp in my ear, accented by a puff of warm air and a quick nip from his teeth on my earlobe followed by a kiss to soothe away the sting.

He was almost completely inside me now, and the sensation was nearly more than I could take. My fingers were digging into the sheets, his back, the pillow, gripping the headboard—whatever they could find to keep me rooted in reality and from drifting away with the overwhelming bliss he was filling me with.

I shamelessly rocked my hips into him, lifting my ass off the bed and hooking my legs around the back of his thighs for leverage to drive myself up and him deeper into me. I pushed through the sensation of my walls widening for him, not caring about anything except getting all of him in me. I hadn't just been talking. I needed every bit of him. Every inch.

18

BRUCE

She was divine. Every thrust into Natasha felt like it was obliterating the memory of any woman who'd ever come before. The nights I'd spent trying to find something meaningful in the arms of someone else were shattered to dust. The wasted time I'd spent with Valerie felt insignificant now. How had I ever thought she was close to good enough? How had I never realized a woman could be so much more, could feel so much more incredible?

I kept my upper body upright with a hand planted on the bed, but freely used my other hand to grip Natasha's breasts, which were the perfect size. They were just big enough to give me a handful and then some, with perky nipples that were constantly at full attention for me. I ran my hand over every bit of her, feeling just as mesmerized by the graceful lines of her neck and hips as I was by the carnal pleasure of her pussy's chokehold on my cock and the soft weight of her breasts. She was an angel. Perfection. Above all, she was *mine*. There was no denying it.

Every last fragment of her attention was on me, and mine was on her. It wasn't just the connection of my cock thrusting deeply into her warmth and wetness or the way her moans were spilling out of her more and more powerfully. It was the feeling that we were forming some kind of seal, a bond, like nothing I'd ever felt.

We had been engaged in a fragile dance for weeks now. There was reluctance and caution on both sides. We'd taken exploratory stabs toward each other, toward something meaningful, but neither of us had been ready to take the full plunge. This was that plunge. Every time I pressed myself into her, the feeling grew. We were building something.

And I wanted to build every angle of it just right, so I gripped her hips and turned her over, flipping her to her stomach and making her get on all fours for me. If the way she let out a low, surprised moan when I slid into her from behind was any sign, she approved.

Her narrow waist formed the sexiest teardrop shape as it spread out into her ass. I gripped her right in the spot where her waist was most narrow, loving the control I felt and how I could yank her into me, using her like my own personal fucktoy. I gave it to her hard from behind, increasing my pace until every thrust was punctuated by the slap of my hips against her supple ass.

She reached up to grip the headboard, and I loved that she couldn't stop turning around to look at me. She wasn't content to close her eyes and imagine. She wanted to *see* me. And I could tell the sight of me fucking her was driving her up the wall, because her eyes couldn't stop flicking from my face to my chest and abs and even my hands on her body.

I reached around her to grip her breasts, which felt even heavier and larger as they hung below her and shook every time I pounded into her.

"I want to see you more," she said breathlessly. She turned around to grip my shoulder and urged me down on the bed so I was on my back.

I'd always preferred to be the one in control, but the way she wanted to initiate this new position was so hot that I didn't care. I loved every second of watching her climb on top of me. She wrapped her hand around my cock, which was absolutely covered in her arousal, and she eased herself down onto me, giving me the most spectacular view of her entire body, from the way her inner thighs were glistening wet to her parted lips that were still bright red from our kisses.

She gasped with relief as she lowered herself down. When she caught me looking back at her as she started bouncing up and down on me, she looked away, cheeks flushing the most perfect shade of red. I reached up to grip her ass, and started moving my hips up to meet her movements. I was close to losing it now. I was so fucking close.

She put one hand on her own breast, and I loved that it seemed unconscious, like she didn't even realize how insanely sexy she was as she fondled herself while she rode me.

She leaned forward then, planting both hands on my chest and finally let loose. She gripped me like a handhold and started humping me shamelessly. I laid back and enjoyed the ride, watching her scrunched forehead and her swaying breasts. It was pure ecstasy, and I knew if I let it go much longer, I was going to cum.

I had spent weeks fantasizing about how I'd fuck her, and every time, it ended with me on top of her. It ended with her small hands digging into my back and her legs wrapped tightly around me like she was clinging on for dear life.

I reached up, planted a hand in the center of her chest, and forced her backwards as I rolled up. Somehow, I managed to keep myself inside her through the shift of positions, and within seconds, I was on top of her. I reached back and pulled her legs up so they were wrapped around my waist and leaned down to kiss her.

Then I let her have it. I didn't hold back anything. I didn't worry about drawing things out or whether she'd cum before I did, because I could feel how close she was. I knew she was on the edge, just like I was.

Her hands dug into my back, and it was the completion of my fantasy. I was exactly where I'd wanted, and I felt my balls tighten as my orgasm reached the final stage. At the same moment, her fingers pressed even harder into me and she cried out.

"I'm cumming."

I felt her walls tense around me, milking my cock like her body wanted to make sure it didn't miss a drop of cum, even though I was wearing a condom. My own cock pulsed, releasing an orgasm that lasted longer and felt more intense than anything I'd ever experienced.

I kissed her once more before slowly sliding out of her and sitting up on my knees. I took in the sight of her, exhausted, spread wide for me, and absolutely soaked.

"You're so fucking beautiful," I said.

She licked her lips and looked down at me, obviously still feeling the aftershocks of her orgasm.

"Any chance you'd be up for a shower?" She asked. "I might need your help cleaning up though. I feel a little weak in the knees right now."

"I was hoping you'd ask," I said.

NATASHA SLEPT OVER AT MY PLACE, AND I GOT READY AS QUIETLY AS I could the following morning. I slipped out of bed in the early hours and spent a great deal of time on my computer once I'd gotten dressed for work. When I finally heard Natasha's bare feet shuffling on the floor, I called for her to sit with me at the kitchen table.

She sat down, looking adorably confused with her hair sticking up on one side and her eyes still puffy and squinted from sleep.

"You're all dressed?" she asked.

"Yes. I did a little work this morning researching a potential employee. I've looked over her body of work and decided she would be an incredible fit for our the team at Galleon."

She looked uncomfortable, like she saw where this was going and was trying to figure out how to politely shut it down. "Bruce... I appreciate it. I really do, but I don't want to be your intern again. I want to be with you, but I don't want to work as some kind of slave getting paid charity money."

"I'm not talking about an internship. I'm talking about a real spot on my team. I've seen that you have a head for this, Natasha. What most of my employees do isn't about having the right college degree or learning the right formulas in school. It's just instinct and what's up here." I tapped my temple. "I read your articles. You have an amazing grasp of the real reasons a business ticks, and that's half the battle with marketing. We can easily teach you the rest."

She frowned, shaking her head and looking down at her hands. "I don't know what to say. I mean, I don't want to sound ungrateful, but I still feel like this is just you finding a way to give me a handout. I know I need it, but it's important to me to earn my way. I never wanted to feel like I was a burden on anybody or like I didn't belong. Besides, my dream was always to be a journalist. I don't even know if I'd like being a marketer or whatever it is you're describing."

"I'm not going to lie to you. I want to give you money. I've wanted to give you money to fix your problems even when I was trying to push you out of my life. I'd never have missed the money it would take to set you up to live happily for years and years in the city, but I knew you were the kind of person who wouldn't take a handout. You're proud and you have integrity. I love that about you. So believe me when I say this isn't a handout. If I had looked over your work and thought you really couldn't do the job, I wouldn't be making you this offer. Would I be going through the trouble of digging through your articles if I didn't know you? No. But that's life. Getting the good jobs is sometimes about who you know, and taking this wouldn't be taking any more of an advantage than half the people living in the city have taken."

I waited.

"*If* I accepted this job, I'd need to know you weren't going to treat me special just because I'm your—"

"Lady of the night?" I suggested.

She gave me a sour look, but then grinned. "I was thinking more along the lines of the 'G' word."

"Hmm. You're going to have to be more specific."

"Girlfriend," she snapped.

I smirked. "Well, if you're going to be so persistent about it, then sure. Also, I need clarification. Is the girlfriend thing a condition of your accepting the position, or is it separate?"

She looked like she was trying to glare a hole straight through me.

"I'm kidding," I said softly. "I already thought of you as my girlfriend, even before yesterday. You were my ex for a little, and now you're my girlfriend again. Okay?"

"Don't I get a say in this?" she asked.

Now it was my turn to glare.

She held up her hands in defense. "Kidding, too. But to answer your question, no, I still want to be your girlfriend with or without the job, obviously. I'm just saying I don't want to be a joke. I don't want everyone looking at me like I screwed my way in. You know?"

"Technically you did bang the boss."

"One of the bosses," she added.

"Good point. Also, make sure it stays that way."

She gave me an amused look. "I think one Chamberson brother is more than enough for me. You have nothing to worry about."

"It does play havoc on the ego. The guy looks exactly like me.

If a woman ever cheated on me with him, what excuse would I have?"

"Well, maybe you don't have to worry about 'a woman' anymore and you can just start worrying about me." She paused for a second after she said it and then covered her face. "God. I'm sorry. I just went too hard, too fast and also implied you had to worry about me cheating on you in the same sentence." Adorably, she flicked one finger up to peek at me from behind her hands.

I was smiling. "For some reason, I'm not sure there's going to be such a thing as too hard or too fast with you. And as far as the cheating goes?" I leaned across the table and beckoned her to lean forward too so I could kiss her. "I'll make sure you don't have any orgasms left to spare for anyone else. I'll have you cumming in the morning, after work, and before bed. You'll be all mine. Every last drop."

She leaned back, tried to rock her chair back on two legs, overbalanced, and started pinwheeling her arms for balance. Her eyes went comically wide and I barely reached out and caught her wrist in time to keep her from falling backwards.

"And," I said. "I guess I'll have to also make sure I keep you alive in between all that."

"Sounds like a plan," she said.

"Which part. The never-ending supply of orgasms, or the keeping you alive part?"

"All the parts."

19

EPILOGUE - NATASHA

One Month Later

❧

I took the job working for Bruce, and I couldn't be happier that I did. I'd spent most of my young adult life thinking I wanted to be a reporter, and maybe I still would somewhere down the line. Working for Galleon made me realize what I had actually been craving was a job where my efforts mattered—something that let me give my fullest and get rewarded when I kicked ass. I didn't want the kind of job where my performance was measured on a checklist or by some predetermined criteria for success. I wanted a job where I could flex my brain and feel like I mattered. I thought journalism was that job, and it still could be someday, but right now, I was finding all that I craved at Galleon.

I met Braeden after work at a company party for *Business Insights*. Bruce was coming later in the evening after his meetings were over. I'd put my official resignation in a day after I accepted Bruce's job offer. Before then, I was still technically available as a freelance reporter, and I could've shown up to search for whatever crummy assignment Hank had lying around. Resignation or not, Hank was kind enough to invite me to the party, which was an annual get-together to celebrate the date *Business Insights* was founded.

They had thrown up cheesy party decorations around the office for the occasion, and the food was as bad as usual. But drinks were drinks, and there was a plentiful supply of champagne, which was a gift Mr. Weinstead always paid for, even if he couldn't be bothered to attend the parties himself.

Braeden wore a tattered black t-shirt and jeans. His hair looked like it had been washed recently, which was always nice.

"Think Bruce is going to give me a hard time when he gets here?" asked Braeden.

We were standing by one of the tables where a dozen champagne bottles and plastic cups were set out. It was a classy combination. Expensive champagne in the kind of plastic cups high school kids liked to drink out of at parties, but no one was too proud to take what they could get here. I hadn't spotted Candace yet, but we had arrived a little early, so I was sure she'd be arriving soon. There were only a handful of people milling around so far, and no one was dancing to the music playing loudly from a pair of speakers.

"Why would he give you a hard time? Because you failed out of the job he tried to give you?"

Braeden closed his eyes like he was about to explain something to someone very simple. "I didn't *fail out*. I realized my talents were wasted at a place like that. A bunch of yes men and corporate jimmies who couldn't get off unless there was a stapler within reach? C'mon, man. You know that's not where I want to end up."

"Of course. And I'm sure it had nothing to do with the fact that you had to wake up at 6:30 in the morning."

"Nothing at all," he said. "But I've got a new thing. It's going to be big this time. Trust me."

"What is it?" I asked.

"Well, I don't want to go into all the details because I'm still in the early stages, but let's just say I've been spending a lot of time watching yoga videos on YouTube."

I raised my eyebrows expectantly, waiting for more. "And?" I asked when he seemed content to say nothing else.

"And let's just say," he added in an obnoxiously cryptic tone. "That New York City is about to have a new high profile yogi."

I tried not to laugh. "Can you even touch your toes?"

"It's not about ability, Nat. That's the first lesson. It's about—and this is a phrase I coined, so make sure you credit me if you use it—*willbility.*"

"Willbility?"

"Yes. The willingness to be able. It's the core of my philosophy."

"Well, uh, I'm glad you're passionate about something else. Again."

"Namaste," he said, clapping his palms together and giving me a half bow.

I would've laughed, but I knew my brother too well. He wasn't kidding. It was something I loved about him, even though it seemed to trap him in an endless string of failures and disappointment. He could pour all his passion and energy into a new project for a few days. For those few days, he was truly happy, because no part of him believed he'd fail. I'd learned to nod along with him and smile because whether he was doomed to fail or not, he was my brother, and he was happy in moments like this. I'd always be crossing my fingers that he would make one of his crazy ideas stick, but until then, I would do what I could: be there for him.

"It sounds amazing," I said cheerily. "Let me know when you're up and running and maybe I can put a good word in for you at Galleon. I'm sure some of the ladies there are into yoga."

"Very good," he said, and I might've imagined it, but I thought he actually spoke with a slight Asian accent.

I covered my mouth so he wouldn't see my smile.

Candace had arrived with a group of people, and she spotted me right away. She did an awkward kind of hands-over-the-head waving wiggle walk toward me. "Natashaaaa!" she growled in a kind of scarily deep voice.

"Candaaace," I said, grinning as I tried to mimic her deep, weird voice.

She squeezed me in a tight hug. As usual, she smelled like flowery shampoo and sunscreen. Candace took skin-care as serious as death, and she never walked outside without a healthy dose of SPF.

"So?" she chirped. "What is it like working at fancy-schmancy Galleon Enterprises? Do they give you a massage break before lunch? Are the toilets gold-plated?"

"No massages during work hours, and the toilets are porcelain just like everywhere else. But the toilet paper is two-ply."

"Shut up!" Candace punctuated her outburst by slapping my shoulder a little harder than I think she meant to.

"Okay?" I said, flinching back and laughing.

"Sorry," she pulled me in and hugged me again. "I feel like I haven't seen you in forever and it's making me all fritzy. Okay, but it's real talk time. When is the wedding? Babies? I need information."

"Believe it or not, we haven't quite discussed those things yet since we've only been back together for a month. He mentioned something about what Halloween costumes we should get for the work party though, so he's at least planning on us being together until October."

Candace silently mouthed the months and counted on her fingers. "Okay, I lost count, but that's a while, right? He's definitely planning on putting a ring on you. Hands down. Or maybe he wants to load you up with a baby first and then make the whole marriage thing like a foregone conclusion."

I held up a hand. "Easy there, killer. I'm just focusing on balancing the part where he's my boss and also the guy who—"

Candace leaned forward and raised her eyebrows in such a lewd way that I couldn't help laughing.

"The guy who *I'm dating*," I said, emphasizing the words so they sounded more platonic than whatever she was imagining. If I was honest though, the truth probably wasn't far from whatever wild, sex-filled fantasy she was imagining. I didn't exactly have a huge frame of reference to go by, but Bruce had to be far above average in his sex drive. The man was a machine, and I'd started to realize my whole sex robot assessment from those early days hadn't been too far off, except that sleeping with him was definitely *not* emotionless. Bruce was so passionate it gave me chills, like every touch was something sacred and every time was new.

"Speaking of..." said Candace from the side of her mouth.

I followed her eyes to where Bruce was walking in. It still amazed me how much he stood out no matter where he was. His height helped, but there was a distinct difference. He wasn't just some guy. Overlooking him was impossible. I'd seen people on the street stare openly at him like they were trying to figure out what movie they'd seen him in. I didn't blame them. He looked like he should have been a household name—the kind of guy you saw on magazine covers at the beach while you waited in line at the grocery store.

I felt a now-familiar rush of pride in knowing he was my man, especially when I saw the way every woman at the party eventually swiveled their heads to stare longingly after him. The way they watched him from the corners of their eyes with parted lips followed by quick, excited whispers to their friends was a universal language. I didn't need to read their lips to know what they were talking about.

They were talking about Bruce. My Bruce. And they were all

probably wondering if they had some kind of remote chance with him, maybe even some of the ones who weren't single.

Bruce shut that down when he reached me and pulled me into a possessive hug, swallowing me up in his big arms and against the warmth of his body. He pulled back and took my face in his hands, planting a gentle kiss on my lips. It was quick, and not the kind of kiss that made people look away uncomfortably in public places. It was the kind that I'd seen before and swooned to watch, because I knew it was the sort of kiss shared between people who adored each other.

"It was my turn to be late for once," he said, letting me go a little, but still keeping his hand on the small of my back, as if he simply didn't want to stop touching me yet. I loved that about him. He couldn't keep his hands off me, and it had done wonders for my confidence.

"Hey now," I said. "I've gotten a lot better about that."

"You have, as long as I'm helping you along."

I smiled and shrugged. "I guess I'll just have to keep you then."

"You say that like you have a choice."

I noticed Candace then, who was watching us like our conversation was a tennis match in the final round at Wimbledon. "Hi," she said breathily, and reached to shake Bruce's hand. "I'm basically Natasha's best friend. Candace. We should get to know each other better, you know, since Natasha and I are such good friends. Unrelated question: are your friends like you?"

Bruce seemed to take her forwardness in stride. "Like me?" he asked calmly.

I cleared my throat and bulged my eyes at Candace a little.

"You know... Perfect? Because that's totally my type, and if you have any friends like that or..."

"I have an identical twin brother, but I wouldn't wish him on my worst enemy."

"Identical twin... Right," she said slowly. "I knew that, because

Natasha and I looked up pictures of you and your brother on G—"

Her words were muffled when I pressed my palm to her mouth. "Candace doesn't know how to stop talking," I said through my teeth. "Does she?" I asked her.

I pulled my hand away.

"She's right," agreed Candace. "I think it's a condition."

"It's fine," said Bruce.

I noticed Braeden chatting up a woman who looked to be in good shape. I had a suspicion he was pitching his bogus business that was confirmed when I saw him clap his hands together and give her a half bow. To my surprise, the woman seemed to be eating it up. I grinned. Good for him.

Hank wandered over to our small group then. "Bruce Chamberson in the flesh, huh?"

"Last time I checked," said Bruce.

"I wanted to apologize, formally. All's fair in journalism, of course, but I'm sorry for the way it became personal."

"No harm done. But I am curious," said Bruce. "What made you think there was even corruption to search out in the first place?"

"At the risk of embarrassing myself and the entire company... It was a clerical error. We had a guy digging through business accounts to search for anything suspicious, and apparently he reported to Mr. Weinstead that your business was claiming unsustainably high expenses. He said it was a clear sign of tax fraud. Turned out he was looking at your expenses for 2017 and your reported gross income for 2014. Don't ask me how he managed that degree of fuck up, but he's been relieved of his job for the carelessness."

"That was it?" I asked. I'd tried to dig the reason for the suspicion out of Hank a few times without any luck.

"That was it," sighed Hank. "Mr. Weinstead just admitted it to me a couple weeks ago, and only because he wanted me to fire the poor kid who made the mistake. I insisted on having a reason so I wasn't just cutting the kid loose in cold blood, and there it was."

"Well," said Bruce. "I can't pretend to be upset. It was a mistake that landed Natasha in my lap." He paused after he spoke and I could've sworn I saw his cheeks start to turn red. "Poor choice of words," he said after clearing his throat. "I'm just glad it happened the way it did."

I reached out and squeezed his hand. "Me too."

"Yeah, yeah," grunted Hank. "Very sweet."

"Now kiss," whispered Candace, who was standing uncomfortably close.

We both gave her a strange look, and she took a step back. "It was just a suggestion. Geez."

20

EPILOGUE - BRUCE

Four Months Later

~

N atasha squeezed my hand and gave me an encouraging
smile. I'd never felt so nervous in my life. Not before I
asked Natasha to move in with me. Not before I bought the
engagement ring I was still holding for the right moment
with her.

This trumped it all.

Valerie had gotten two DUI's in as many months, and child
protective services started an investigation on her that turned up
several other red flags. Valerie had cocaine in the house, and
she'd also apparently developed a dependency on heavy-duty
painkillers after her last round of plastic surgery. Essentially, CPS
had proved she was highly neglectful and managed to prove it in
court, which meant Caitlyn was being removed from her care.
Valerie had a boyfriend, but he wanted nothing to do with
custody of Caitlyn, and even if he did, the court would've been
reluctant to hand her over to someone who would keep her in the

same neglectful environment. Valerie's parents didn't want her, either.

Legally speaking, I hardly had any more right to adopt Caitlyn than Joe Schmoe off the street, but I had made sure to take all the proper steps to get myself in the front of the line. It helped that Caitlyn had signed a written statement saying she'd like to be adopted by me as a foster child. It also helped that I had the financial means to support her, as well as a clean record.

All that being said, waiting to get word back on whether the situation would be allowed or not had been a nail-biting experience. I would absolutely adopt her whenever the day came that the court decided to completely strip Valerie of her legal right to provide for Caitlyn. I would've liked to think there was a distant chance of Valerie reforming and coming back to be the mother Caitlyn deserved, but somehow I knew that wasn't going to happen.

Today was the day we took her home.

A car pulled up outside my building exactly at the time they said it would. The driver got out to open Caitlyn's door. I thought she might have mixed feelings, given the circumstances, but her face instantly split into a smile when she saw me.

"Thank you," she said into my stomach as she hugged me tightly.

I didn't know what to say. I didn't want to tell her I felt so happy I could burst, because the only reason she'd wound up in my care was that her mother was absolute shit to her. I felt partly to blame for that, too. I wasn't sure how much Valerie would've spiraled out of control if I hadn't kept feeding her the money she demanded out of me. At the same time, I wasn't sure constant legal battles wouldn't have taken their toll, either.

Instead of saying anything, I just hugged her back and then led her inside. Her little hand was in my left, and my right was around Natasha's shoulder.

One Week Later

WILLIAM SAT ON MY COUCH WITH AN AMUSED LOOK ON HIS FACE. He was tossing an expensive paperweight from the end table carelessly up and then snatching it out of the air again and again. Natasha and Caitlyn were playing some card game with endlessly complicated rules. They were on their knees in front of the coffee table, both wearing extremely serious expressions as they were no doubt trying desperately to win.

The two girls were more competitive than I would've believed, and as far as I could tell, they'd immediately hit it off. It helped that they were both apparently obsessed with board games and card games.

"You know," said William. "I'm almost jealous. Really, I am. It must be hard to be done with the exciting part of your life. No more worrying about whether you still look good with your shirt off. No worrying about which hot girl to take home at the end of the night. All those problems... Just *shwip*. Right off the table. Must be nice."

"It is, actually," I said.

He flicked his eyebrows up. "Never me, bro. Never me. I'll happily enjoy your little dysfunctional family second-hand. That's more than enough of a dose of the boring life for me."

"You'll have your day," I said. "Your problem is you haven't met the right girl yet."

"He's right," said Natasha, but she sounded distracted, and she didn't look up from her cards.

"Did you teach her that? Nice trick."

I glared at him. "You remember who used to always win when we fought? Be careful what you say or you'll get a reminder."

"Yeah, yeah. I get it. You don't have to get all worked up over there. I'm just trying to say you did a good job."

"Well thank you, I think."

"You're welcome, I think."

"Boys are so weird," said Caitlyn.

"Especially those two," said Natasha.

"Ouch," said William. "I guess she's not so well-trained after all."

Natasa gave me a wicked little smile that no one else caught. It was a smile that said so much more than words ever could. It said he was right. Natasha would never be the tame housewife or anything close to typical. She was my accident-prone, highly unpredictable, feisty little firecracker, and I knew I wouldn't be able to wait much longer to get on one knee for her.

"That's why I love her," I said.

No one but Natasha and I felt the shockwaves of those words. We hadn't said our "I love you's" yet, and they were words I'd never taken lightly.

"I love you, too," she said, finally seeming to lose focus on her game of cards completely.

"If you guys are going to start making out, I'm leaving," said William.

"Me too," said Caitlyn, but the smirk on her face said she still liked having parents—even if they were her adoptive parents—who knew how to show healthy affection for each other.

"Then get the hell out," I growled.

The two got up and half-ran out of the room, leaving me to pull Natasha up from her knees and onto my lap, where we sank back into the couch.

"I was about to win, you know," she said, eyes heavy and lusty as she scanned my face.

I glanced up at the clock behind her and saw it was ten in the morning. "Well," I said suddenly, gently and carefully shoving her to the side to plop on her ass as I stood up. "Sorry to break the magic, but," I nodded my head to the clock. "It's time for my pre-lunch banana. So... Raincheck?"

"Raincheck my ass," she said, grinning wide as she tugged on me and pulled me back toward the couch.

"Hmm," I said, studying her body and her alluring eyes. "I guess I can postpone the banana."

"I can't," she said, and she leaned forward to take my zipper between her lips. This time, she had enough practice under *my* belt to get it down on the first try.

"This is why I love you."

"The only reason?" she asked, running her palms up my thighs.

"Hell no," I said, suddenly serious. I wanted what she was about to give me, but it could wait. I urged her to stand, taking her by the cheeks and staring down into her eyes. "I love you because you never cared who I was. You never cared that I had money or that I was the boss. You were always yourself, even if you did hide the reason you were my intern. You're the most genuine person I know, and that means I love *you,* not some mask you wore to impress me."

She narrowed her eyes, a faint smile forming on her face. "Is this your nice way of saying I don't give good head?"

I laughed. "No. It's my nice way of saying I don't only love you because you are phenomenal between the sheets."

"Hmm. I accept." She leaned in and kissed my neck. "And since we're being mushy, I should say that I always appreciated how you let me show what I was capable of. Everybody else in my life immediately wrote me off because I was clumsy and a screw-up, which, admittedly, isn't that unreasonable. But you always looked past that."

"And you are capable."

She got back on her knees and smiled up at me with a look absolutely dripping with mischief. "How about we take a walk down memory lane? Maybe we can start where it all began..."

PLEASE DON'T FORGET TO LEAVE A REVIEW!

Thank you so much for reading! Whether you loved the book or not, it would mean the world to me if you left an honest review on Amazon. I read every single review and take them all to heart, even on older books, so it's not just a great way to give me your feedback and help me improve, it's also one of the best ways to support me and help me find new readers.

I also hope those of you who have been reading with me since the beginning didn't mind the little departure from my normally serious and sometimes dark tone. The last few months have been a little bit darker for me, and it felt like a book that didn't take itself so seriously would be the perfect medicine.

JOIN MY MAILING LIST

Join my mailing list to get regular updates from me on my upcoming projects, opportunities to earn gift cards and prizes, bonus content, and more!

Hate the spam? Join my "Bloom Only" newsletter for a monthly update when my newest book is live and absolutely no additional emails!

Check out my website for my bi-weekly blog posts and more

behind-the-scenes information about me, my books, and the author world than you'll know what to do with!

You can also find me on Facebook. I love to interact with fans, post sneak peeks for my upcoming books, host giveaways, and hear feedback!

ALSO BY PENELOPE BLOOM

My Most Recent Books
   Hate at First Sight (Coming back to Amazon this August! Keep an eye out for it)
   Baby for the Beast
   Baby for the Brute
   Savage (#20 ranked Amazon bestselling novel for February)
   The Dom's Bride (#40 ranked Amazon bestselling novel for January)

(Babies for the Doms)
   Knocked Up and Punished (top 21 Best Seller)
   Knocked Up by the Master (top 12 Best Seller)
   Knocked Up by the Dom (USA Today Bestselling Novel and #8 ranked Bestseller)

(The Citrione Crime Family)

His (Book 1)
Mine (Book 2)
Dark (Book 3)

~

Punished (top 40 Best Seller)

Single Dad Next Door (top 12 Best Seller)
The Dom's Virgin (top 22 Best Seller)
Punished by the Prince (top 28 Best Seller)
Single Dad's Virgin (top 10 Best Seller)
Single Dad's Hostage (top 40 Best Seller)
The Bodyguard
Miss Matchmaker

Made in the USA
San Bernardino, CA
10 August 2018